FAMILY
LIFE

FAMILY LIFE

A NOVEL

Akhil Sharma

ff

FABER & FABER

First published in the United States in 2014 by
W. W. Norton & Company, Inc.
500 Fifth Avenue, New York, NY 10110

First published in the UK in 2014 by
Faber & Faber Limited
Bloomsbury House
74–77 Great Russell Street
London WC1B 3DA

Printed and bound by CPI Group (UK) Ltd, Croydon, CR0 4YY

A CIP record for this book
is available from the British Library

ISBN 978–0–571–31426–3 (hardback edition)

ISBN 978–0–571–22453–1 (export edition)

FSC
www.fsc.org
MIX
Paper from
responsible sources
FSC® C101712

2 4 6 8 10 9 7 5 3 1

This book is dedicated to my beloved wife Lisa Swanson;
my poor brother Anup Sharma; and my brave and faithful parents
Pritam and Jai Narayan Sharma

FAMILY
LIFE

My father has a glum nature. He retired three years ago, and he doesn't talk much. Left to himself, he can remain silent for days. When this happens, he begins brooding, he begins thinking strange thoughts. Recently he told me that I was selfish, that I had always been selfish, that when I was a baby I would start to cry as soon as he turned on the TV. I am forty and he is seventy-two. When he said this, I began tickling him. I was in my parents' house in New Jersey, on a sofa in their living room. "Who's the sad baby?" I said. "Who's the baby that cries all the time?"

"Get away," he squeaked, as he fell back and tried to wriggle away. "Stop being a joker. I'm not kidding." My father is a sort of golden color. Skin hangs loosely from beneath his chin. He has long thin earlobes the way some old people have.

My mother is more cheerful than my father. "Be like me," she often tells him. "See how many friends I have? Look how I'm always smiling." But my mother gets unhappy too, and when she does, she sighs and says, "I'm bored. What is this life we lead? Where is Ajay? What was the point of having raised him?"

As far back as I can remember my parents have bothered each other.

In India we lived in two cement rooms on the roof of a two story house in Delhi. The bathroom stood separate from the living quarters. It had a sink attached to the outside of one of the walls. Each night my father would stand before the sink, the sky full of stars, and brush his teeth till his gums bled. Then, he would spit the blood into the sink and turn to my mother and say, "Death, Shuba, death. No matter what we do, we will all die."

"Yes, yes, beat drums," my mother said once. "Tell the newspapers, too. Make sure everyone knows this thing you have discovered." Like many people of her generation, those born before Independence, my mother viewed gloom as unpatriotic. To complain was to show that one was not willing to accept difficulties; that one was not willing to do the hard work that was needed to build the country.

My father is two years older than my mother. Unlike her, he saw dishonesty and selfishness everywhere. Not only did he see these things but he believed that everybody else did, too, and that they were deliberately not acknowledging what they saw.

My mother's irritation at his spitting blood, he interpreted as hypocrisy.

· · ·

M<small>Y FATHER WAS</small> an accountant. He went to the American consulate and stood in the line that circled around the courtyard. He submitted his paperwork for a visa.

My father had wanted to emigrate to the West ever since he was in his early twenties, ever since America liberalized its immigration policies in 1965. His wish was born out of self-loathing. Often when he walked down a street in India, he would feel that the buildings he passed were indifferent to him, that he mattered so little to them that he might as well not have been born. Because he attributed this feeling to his circumstances and not to the fact that he was the sort of person who sensed buildings having opinions of him, he believed that if he were somewhere else, especially somewhere where he earned in dollars and so was rich, he would be a different person and not feel the way he did.

Another reason he wanted to emigrate was that he saw the West as glamorous with the excitement of science. In India in the fifties, sixties, and seventies, science felt very much like magic. I remember that when we turned on the radio, first the voices would sound far away and then they would rush at us, and this created the sense of the machine making some special effort just for us.

Of everybody in my family, my father loved science the most. The way he tried to bring it into his life was by going to medical clinics and having his urine tested. Of course, hypochondria had something to do with this; my father felt that there was something wrong with him and perhaps this was a simple thing that a doctor could fix. Also, when he sat in the clinics and talked to doctors in lab coats, he felt that he was close to important things, that what the doctors were doing was the same as what doctors would do in England or Germany or America, and so he was already there in those foreign countries.

To understand the glamour of science, it is important to remember that the sixties and seventies were the era of the Green Revolution. Science seemed the most important thing in the world. Even I, as a child of five or six, knew that because of the Green Revolution there was now fodder in the summer and so people who would have died were now saved. The Green Revolution was effecting everything. I heard my mother discuss soy recipes with neighbors and talk about how soy was as good as cheese. All over Delhi, Mother Dairy was putting up its cement kiosks with the blue drop on the side. That the Green Revolution had come from the West, that organizations like the Ford Foundation had brought it to us without expectations of gain or payment, made the West seem a place for great goodness. I personally think that all the anti-Western movies of the seventies like *Haré Rama, Haré Krishna* and *Purab aur Pachhim* sprang not from the unease of hippies arriving but from our sense of inferiority before the munificence of the West.

My mother had no interest in emigrating for herself. She was a high school teacher of economics, and she liked her job. She said that teaching was the best job possible, that one received respect and one learned things as well as taught them. Yet my mother was aware that the West would provide me and my brother with opportunities. Then came the Emergency. After Indira Gandhi suspended the constitution and put thousands of people in jail, my parents, like nearly everyone, lost faith in the government. Before then, my parents, even my father, were proud enough of India being independent that when they saw a cloud, they would think, *That's an Indian cloud.* After the Emergency, they began to feel that even though they were ordinary and not likely to get into trouble with the government, it might still be better to leave.

In 1978, my father left for America.

IN AMERICA, MY father began working as a clerk for a government agency. He rented an apartment in a place called Queens, New York. A year after he left us, he sent airplane tickets.

The Delhi of the seventies is hard to imagine: the quietness, the streets empty of traffic, children playing cricket in the middle of the street and rarely having to move out of the way to let cars by, the vegetable vendors who came pushing their carts down the street in the late afternoon, crying out their wares in tight, high-pitched voices. There weren't VCRs back then, let alone cable channels. A movie would play for twenty-five or fifty weeks in huge auditorium theaters, and then once the movie was gone, it was gone forever. I remember feeling grief when the enormous billboards for *Sholay* at the end of our street were taken down. It was like somebody had died.

It is also hard to remember how frugal we were. We saved the cotton that comes inside pill bottles. Our mothers used it to make wicks. This frugality meant that we were sensitive to the physical reality of our world in a way most people no longer are. When my mother bought a box of matches, she had my brother sit at a table and use a razor to split the matches in half. When we had to light several things, we would use the match to set a twist of paper on fire and then walk around the apartment lighting the stove, the incense stick, the mosquito coil. This close engagement with things meant that we were conscious that the wood of a match is soft, that a bit of spit on paper slows down how it burns.

By the time our airplane tickets arrived, not every family hired a band to play outside their house on the day of the departure to a foreign country. Still, many families did.

It was afternoon when the tickets came. My brother and I were in the living room playing Snakes and Ladders. The light was dim from the curtains that had been drawn to keep out the heat. When we heard shouts from the street, we knew it had to be the tickets.

Birju and I climbed out onto the balcony that connected

our apartment's two rooms. Below us the street shimmered with August heat. I was eight at the time and Birju twelve. Five or six children my own age or even younger were walking in our direction. Leading them was a skinny sunburnt young man and a fat gray-haired woman in pantaloons and a baggy shirt. Children kept breaking away from the group. Every house on our street had boundary walls, topped with shards of glass. These walls were broken with iron gates, and the children stopped before the gates and shouted, "Shuba auntie's tickets have come." I had never heard us shouted about before. I became excited. I smiled. I wanted to shout and wave that we were home.

Behri auntie, the fat woman leading the crowd, was a neighbor. Almost anybody who was not a relative but toward whom we had to show respect was an "auntie" or "uncle." I knew Behri auntie didn't like us and was coming just to be present when the tickets arrived so later she could say she was there. The thin man was the messenger. He walked proudly, his head high, not acknowledging the children following him. He was holding a large manila envelope in one hand.

Birju and I on the balcony flattened ourselves into the little shade that lay along the wall. Birju looked down at the street and muttered, "Everybody becomes your friend when you're going to America." He had curly hair and a round fat chin that seemed to lengthen his face with its weight. Hearing him, my pride at being shouted about turned to embarrassment. Both my brother and my mother had a way of speaking that made them sound as if they knew secret things. People might be able to fool themselves and each other, but my brother and mother could look into them and see the truth. My brother had another thing that gave him an air of authority. He was ranked first in his class, and as happens in such cases, everybody in our neighborhood treated him as special. Because of his good grades, he appeared to be somebody who had a destiny. There was a sense with Birju that he was already connected to the wider world. When he passed judgment, it felt like when the radio made an announcement and one felt that whatever one had heard had to be correct.

"Your mouth drips poison," I said.

A few minutes later, the crowd arrived in our living room. Behri auntie sat down panting on a stool.

"Well, Shuba," she said, "at last you are getting your wish."

My mother had been napping and her hair was loose. She was wearing a wrinkled cotton sari. Silently she examined the tickets, which looked like checkbooks. The messenger stood before her, and the children who had come with Behri were scattered around the dim space, writing their names on the luggage tags that the messenger had brought.

When my mother didn't reply, Behri said, "Your mister must be very happy, too." Even I knew that there was something improper about the word "mister." In those shy days, when even husbands and wives never touched in public, to wander out of Hindi was to suggest that something indecent was being referred to.

"Mishraji will be happy to see Birju and Ajay," my mother said, and her using my father's last name with a "ji" attached signaled that we could not be accused of indecency.

"He will be happy to see you, too. He's been away for a year." After Behri said this, there was a lingering silence. I wasn't sure of the meaning of all that was being exchanged, but I understood that some battle was occurring.

"Happy, Shuba?" Behri said, as if to confirm her victory.

"Why shouldn't I be happy?" my mother asked sounding irritated.

Confronted, Behri looked away.

In the silence that followed, the messenger leaned toward my mother. He whispered, "Reward, reward." He used the Urdu word "inam," as if to turn the giving of a tip into something Mughal and aristocratic.

The idea of tipping for ordinary services had only recently entered India. Nobody wanted to tip, though, and so everyone looked for nonblameworthy ways to avoid doing so. Tipping was therefore often condemned as Muslim or a foreign affectation.

Behri heard the "inam" and, wanting to be angry at someone, whipped her head toward the messenger. "Inam? That's not the sort of neighborhood you have come to, Brother. We are ordinary people. We don't speak English. We don't wear blue jeans. We don't drink wine and have three wives."

Birju, like me, enjoyed bullying people, especially when he could get away with it. Seeing that an adult was harassing the

messenger and since a messenger is poor and not a regular visi-
tor, he, too, joined in chiding the man. "Reward! Brother, have
you caught a bandit? Have you caught a fugitive? Can I ask
this? If you have, we'll make sure the police give you a reward."

My mother, after her fight, was not now going to agree with
anything Behri said. Though she, too, hated tipping, she said,
"Ajay, go get my purse." I left and went to our bedroom. The
armoire where my mother kept the purse was in there. I came
back after a moment with the bag.

The messenger took the one rupee coin. He touched it to
his forehead.

Once he was gone, Behri said, "Shuba, you are already
American."

Then she pushed herself off the stool. She turned to the
children. "Come, come. Go home."

AT FIRST having the tickets thrilled me.

The next morning, I went to the milk shop at the end of
our street. The shop was a cement booth about as wide as a
ticket counter. It was a hot, bright morning and I was sweating by the time I arrived. The air near the shop smelled of
milk and spoilage and the incense that the milkman burned
every morning as part of his prayers. There was a crush of
boys on the sidewalk, spilling off it onto the road, holding

up their milk pails, calling out, "Brother, Brother," to get the milkman's attention.

Some of the boys looked at me and glanced away, their heads turning like oscillating table fans. Others glared as if I had taken something from them. To me, both reactions showed jealousy, and they thrilled me.

I came up to a boy and pressed my hands together before me. "Namaste," I said. The boy looked at me strangely. I knew it was odd to speak so formally to someone my own age, but I felt that being excessively proper would make me even more special; not only was I going to America, but I was polite and humble. "How is your family? Everybody happy? Healthy?" Speaking increased my excitement. I tried not to smile. I took out a luggage tag from the pocket of my short pants. The tag had an elastic loop coming out of a small hole. "Our tickets arrived. We got these also. Do you want to see?" I held out the tag.

The boy was boxed in. If he refused to look, he would be revealing his jealousy and so appear weak. He took the tag. After handling it for a moment, he gave it back in silence.

I spoke again. "I learned that everybody in America has their own speedboat." Nobody had told me any such thing. As I said this, though, it felt true. "Brother, I can't swim. I hope I don't drown." To be modest and to also be leaving for America made me feel like I was wonderful.

The crowd shuffled. The boy I was talking to moved away. I turned to another boy and pressed my hands together once more.

. . .

THE SUNDAY AFTER the tickets arrived, my mother took me and Birju to see my grandparents. She shook us awake while it was still dark. We went out onto the roof and bathed using a bucket and a mug. It was strange to bathe with the moon above us. And when the horizon began to brighten that first light felt rare and precious. And then, a little later, as the sky brightened, we walked down the street toward the bus stand. Birju walked beside my mother and I walked in the shadow of the boundary walls. In the shade, the dust was heavier and things smelled different, as if a fragment of the night lingered.

Everything about where my grandparents lived was pleasingly miniature. Their lane was so narrow I could reach out and touch the houses on both sides. In the morning, when we arrived, the gutters ran with soapy water and the lane smelled of soap and also of hot oil and dough from the parathas being fried.

My grandfather, seeing us, straightened up from sweeping his small whitewashed courtyard. "Who are these two princes? Are they saints who have come to bless my house?" He wore white pajamas and a homemade sleeveless undershirt with long shoulder straps. I hurried forward and to show that I was good and knew to display respect, touched his feet.

"We have gotten our airplane tickets, nanaji," Birju said. Hearing this, I wished I had said it so that then I would be the one bringing the news.

"I'm not letting both of you go. One of you I will keep."

"We'll miss you," Birju said, reaching down to touch our grandfather's feet. He had long, bony arms.

"I will miss you, too," I murmured, again feeling jealous that Birju had said something that made him look good.

There were small rooms on two sides of the courtyard. These were cool, shadowy places. They smelled of mothballs, and this was pleasant because it suggested closed trunks and things that would be revealed when the seasons changed.

Around eleven that morning, I fell asleep on a cot in one of the rooms. When I woke, Birju was lying next to me, smelling of the coconut oil that my mother put into his hair because of his dandruff. My mother and grandmother were sitting on the floor near the courtyard. They were talking in whispers and making seemi, rubbing wads of dough between their fingers so that the dough became thin as a thread, then pinching off small pieces so that these fell on the towels spread in their laps. The seemi looked like fingernail clippings.

"You don't speak English," my grandmother whispered.

"I will learn."

"You're almost forty."

"I'm going for Birju and Ajay."

"Isn't it better for them to be here with their whole family?"

"Their father is there."

"Here you have a job."

"What is here? Thieves? That Indira woman will eat us."

I lay on my side and watched and listened. Usually, naps left me melancholy. Lying there, I began to think that when I was in America, I wouldn't be able to see my grandparents every Sunday. Till then, I had not fully understood that going to America meant leaving India. I had somehow imagined that I would get to have the jet packs and chewing gum that people in America had and also be able to show these things off to my friends.

Soon it was time for lunch. I sat on the floor beside Birju. I broke off pieces of roti and leaned forward so that whatever dripped would fall onto the steel plate before me. The melancholy wouldn't go away. I couldn't quite believe that when I left India, my grandparents' house would continue to exist, that the gutters along the sides of the lane would still run with soapy water.

We were supposed to leave in early October. In August, this seemed far away. Then September arrived. Every evening I had the sense that the day had rushed by, that I had not done enough and the day had been wasted.

I started to talk in my sleep. Most afternoons when I got home from school, Birju and my mother and I napped on a wide bed in the bedroom. The thick curtains would be pulled shut, the ceiling fan spinning. There would be trays of water on the floor to soften the air. One afternoon, I lay on the bed with my eyes open. I couldn't move my arms and legs. I was hot, sweating, panicked. I saw ants carrying our television up a wall. I said, "The red ants are carrying away the TV." Birju was sitting beside me looking down, appearing amused. He seemed more real than the ants.

In school, I started getting into fights. I was in third grade. One afternoon, I was standing in the back of my class, talking with my best friend Hershu and a little Sikh boy whose hair was pulled into a bun under a black cloth. The Sikh boy said, "Americans clean themselves with paper, not water."

"I know that," I said. "Say something that other people don't know."

"In America they say 'yeah' not yes. Mrs. Singh told me to let you know."

"That's nothing. On an airplane, the stewardess has to give you whatever you ask for. I'm going to ask for a baby tiger."

"When you get on the plane, go to the back," Hershu said. "Go all the way to the back to sit." Hershu said this softly. He had a large head, which looked too big for his body. "When an aeroplane falls, it falls with its front down."

"Get away, evil-eyed one," I exclaimed. I put my hands on Hershu's chest and shoved. He stumbled back. He stared at me for a moment. His eyes got wet.

"Look," I called out, "he's going to cry."

Hershu turned away and walked to his seat. I couldn't understand why I had just done this thing.

. . .

I CONTINUED GOING TO the milk shop every morning. Because I would be emigrating to America, the milkman did not have me wait in the crowd and instead called me to the front. He probably did this because bestowing attention was one of his few powers.

Once he said, "What will happen to your brother's bicycle?" The milkman was seventeen or eighteen, and he was in the shop's entrance, his pajamas rolled up, barefoot because milk inevitably got spilled and it is a sin to step on milk with slippers.

"I don't know."

"Tell your mother I would like to buy it."

As he spoke, I was conscious of all the boys watching. I felt their eyes on the back of my neck like hot sun.

Relatives started coming to the apartment and asking for the things that might be left behind.

One warm night, my father's younger brother visited. He sat on the sofa in the living room glowering, sweat dripping from his mustache. The ceiling fan spun. He drank several cups of tea. Finally he said, "What are you going to do with the television and refrigerator?"

"Ji, we were planning to sell it," my mother answered.

"Why? Don't you have enough money?"

Piece by piece, furniture vanished. The easy chairs disappeared, the daybed was taken away, and the sofa faced a blank wall before it, too, was gone. Laborers, thin as mice, came wearing torn shirts, smelling of dried sweat, sheets wrapped around their waists. One laborer tilted the iron armoire that stood in the living room onto another laborer's back. The burdened man inched out of the room. The dining table was turned onto its side and carried away. Once the table was gone, there were white scuff marks on the cement floor where it had stood. When even the TV was gone, Birju and I stood in a corner of the empty living room and called out "Oh! Oh!" to stir up echoes.

Near the end of September, Birju convinced me that I was walking and talking in my sleep because I was possessed by a ghost.

This happened late one afternoon. Birju and I had just woken from our nap, and we were sitting on the bed drinking our daily glass of milk with rose syrup. Birju said, "Ajay, don't tell Mommy this, but you are possessed. When you talk, it isn't you talking but the ghost."

"You're lying. You're always lying."

"I talked to the ghost, and he said that he had the gift of prophecy."

I had always believed that I might possess supernatural powers, like flying or maybe seeing into the future. "You're lying," I said, hoping that he was right.

"I asked him what was going to happen to me." Birju said this and stopped. He looked serious.

"What did the ghost say?"

"He said I'm going to die."

I stared at my brother. He looked down. He had long eyelashes and narrow shoulders and a narrow chest.

"I didn't believe him. I said, 'If you're a ghost, why do you sound like Ajay?' He said, 'Since I haven't been born again, I haven't committed any sins, and so I have a child's innocence.'"

"Maybe the ghost was lying."

"Why would he lie?"

I was quiet for a moment. Birju appeared to have the truth on his side. I asked, "Did the ghost say anything about me?"

"Why should I ask about you? I have my own problems."

BIRJU SOBBED WHEN his bicycle was taken away. He refused to go downstairs to watch it being put into the back of a truck. Instead, he sat on the living room floor with the heels of his hands pressed into his eyes.

Among the things that remained was my plastic bucket of toys. My mother said that I could just leave it behind in the apartment. The thought of the yellow bucket standing alone in the empty living room, the apartment locked, made me feel guilty, like I would be abandoning it. I decided to give away my toys.

On our last morning in India, I took the bucket with me to the milk shop. When I saw the crowd of boys, shoving and pushing on the sidewalk, I felt embarrassed. I wanted the boys to remember me, and yet in the past, I had tried to make them feel bad.

"Will you take something?" I said, standing on the sidewalk and speaking to a boy whose head was covered in stubble. I took a little car from the bucket and held it out. My voice trembled. "I'm going away and perhaps you would like to have it."

The boy's hand struck my palm. As soon as it did, I wanted my car back.

"Would you like something else?" I said, my voice shaking. I put the bucket down and stepped away. The boy bent and hurriedly searched through it. He took out two plastic soldiers, a horse, and a large see-through plastic gun that made a noise and flashed light when the trigger was pulled.

I moved to another boy. I knew this boy was poor since, instead of bringing a milk pail to the shop, he brought a cup.

Soon the bucket was empty. I didn't know what to do with the bucket. "Will you take it?" I asked the poor boy. He nodded shyly. As I was leaving, the milk man cried, "Remember me in America."

That night, my mother's younger brother arrived to take us to the airport.

I used to think that my father had been assigned to us by the government. This was because he appeared to serve no purpose. When he got home in the evening, all he did was sit in his chair in the living room, drink tea, and read the paper. Often he looked angry. By the time we left for America, I knew that the government had not sent him to live with us. Still, I continued to think he served no purpose. Also, I found him frightening.

My father was waiting for us in the arrivals hall at the airport. He was leaning against a metal railing and he appeared angry. I saw him and got anxious.

The apartment my father had rented had one bedroom. It was in a tall, brown-brick building in Queens. The apartment's gray metal front door swung open into a foyer with a wooden floor. Beyond this was a living room with a reddish brown carpet that went from wall to wall. Other than in the movies, I had never seen a carpet. Birju and my parents walked across the foyer and into the living room. I went to the carpet's edge and stopped. A brass metal strip held it to the floor. I took a step forward. I felt as if I were stepping onto a painting. I tried not to bring my weight down.

My father took us to the bathroom to show us toilet paper and hot water. While my mother was interested in status, being better educated than others or being considered more proper, my father was just interested in being rich. I think this was because although both of my parents had grown up poor, my father's childhood had been much more desperate. At some point my grandfather, my father's father, had begun to believe that thorns were growing out of his palms. He had taken a razor and picked at them till they were shaggy with scraps of skin. Because of my grandfather's problems, my father had grown up feeling that no matter what he did, people would look down on him. As a result, he cared less about convincing people of his merits and more about just owning things.

The bathroom was narrow. It had a tub, sink, and toilet in a row along one wall. My father reached between Birju and me to turn on the tap. Hot water came shaking and steaming from the faucet. He stepped back and looked at us to gauge our reaction.

I had never seen hot water coming from a tap before. In India, during winter, my mother used to get up early to heat pots of water on the stove so we could bathe. Watching the hot water spill as if water being hot meant nothing, as if there was an endless supply, I had the sense of being in a fairy tale, one of those stories with a jug that is always full of milk or a bag that never empties of food.

During the coming days, the wealth of America kept astonishing me. The television had programming from morning till night. I had never been in an elevator before and when I pressed a button in the elevator and the elevator started moving, I felt powerful that it had to obey me. In our shiny brass mailbox in the lobby, we received ads on colored paper. In India colored paper could be sold to the recycler for more money than newsprint. The sliding glass doors of our apartment building would open when we approached. Each time this happened, I felt that we had been mistaken for somebody important.

Outside our building was a four-lane road. This was usually full of cars, and every few blocks there were traffic lights. In India, the only traffic light I had ever seen was near India Gate. My parents had taken me and Birju for picnics near there, and when they did, we would go look at the light. People were so unused to being directed by a light that a traffic guard in a white uniform and white pith helmet stood underneath, repeating its directions with his hands.

My father, who had seemed pointless in India, had brought us to America, and made us rich. What he had done was undeniable. He now seemed mysterious, like he was a different person, someone who looked like my father but was not the same man.

All the time now my father said things that revealed him as knowledgeable, as someone who could not just be ignored. My mother, Birju, and I had decided that a hot dog was made from dog meat. We had even discussed what part of a dog a hot dog must be made of. We had agreed that it had to be a tail. Then my father came home and heard us and started laughing.

Until we arrived in America, my mother had been the one who made all the decisions about Birju and me. Now I realized that my father, too, had plans for us. This felt both surprising and intrusive, like having my cheeks pinched by a relative I did not know.

He took Birju and me to a library. I had been in two libraries till then. One had had newspapers but not books and was used primarily by people searching employment ads. This had been a small, noisy room next to a barbershop. The other had been on the second floor of a temple, and one had to pay to join. This had had books, but these were kept locked in glass-fronted cabinets.

The library in Queens was bigger than either of the two I had seen. It had several rooms, and they were long, with many metal shelves. The library had thousands of books, and the librarian said we could check out as many as we wanted. At first, I did not believe her.

My father told Birju and me that he would give us fifty cents for each book we read. This bribing struck me as un-Indian and wrong. My mother had told us that Americans were afraid of demanding things from their children. She said this was because American parents did not care about their children and were unwilling to do the hard thing of disciplining them. If my father wanted us to read, what he should have done was threaten to beat us. I wondered whether my father might have become too American during the year that he was living alone. It seemed typical of him to choose to identify with wealthy Americans instead of the propriety of India.

I wanted to take out ten picture books.

My father said, "You think I'm going to give you money for such small books?"

Along with Birju and me reading, the other thing my father wanted was for Birju to get into a school called the Bronx High School of Science, where the son of one of his colleagues had been accepted.

My MOTHER, BIRJU, and I had taken everything we could from the airplane: red Air India blankets, pillows with paper pillowcases, headsets, sachets of ketchup, packets of salt and pepper, air-sickness bags. Birju and I slept on mattresses on the living room floor, and we used the blankets until they frayed and tore. Around the time that they did, we started going to school.

At school I sat at the very back of the class, in the row closest to the door. Often I couldn't understand what my teacher was saying. I had studied English in India, but either my teacher spoke too quickly and used words I didn't know, or I was so afraid that her words sounded garbled to my ears.

It was strange to be among so many whites. They all

looked alike. When a boy came up to me between periods and asked a question, it took me a moment to realize I had spoken to him before.

We had lunch in an asphalt yard surrounded by a high chain-link fence. Wheeled garbage cans were spread around the yard. I was often bullied. Sometimes a little boy would come up to me and tell me that I smelled bad. Then, if I said anything, a bigger boy would appear so suddenly that I couldn't tell where he had come from. He would knock me down. He'd stand over me, fists clenched, and demand, "You want to fight? You want to fight?"

Sometimes boys surrounded me and shoved me back and forth, keeping me upright as a kind of game.

Often, standing in a corner of the asphalt yard, I would think, *There has been a mistake. I am not the sort of boy who is pushed around. I am good at cricket. I am good at marbles.*

On Diwali, it was odd to go to school, odd and painful to stand outside the brown brick building waiting for its doors to open. In India, everything would be closed for the festival. All of us children would be home dressed in good clothes—clothes that were too nice to play in, and yet by the afternoon, we would be outside doing just that. Now, in America, standing on the sidewalk, I imagined India, with everyone home for the new year. At that moment, I felt the life I was living in America was not important, that no matter how rich America was, how wonderful it was to have cartoons on TV, only life in India mattered.

One day a blue aerogramme came from one of Birju's friends, a boy who had not been smart or especially popular. I read the letter and couldn't understand why this boy got to be in India while I was here.

At school I was so confused that everything felt jumbled. The school was three stories tall, with hallways that looped on themselves and stairways connecting the floors like a giant game of Snakes and Ladders. Not only could I not tell white people apart, but I often got lost trying to find my classroom. I worried how, at the end of the day, I would find the stairway to take me down to the door from which I knew the way home. Within a few months, I became so afraid of getting lost in the vastness of the school that I wouldn't leave the classroom when I had to use the toilet. I imagined that if I left, I might end up wandering the hallways and not be able to get back to my class. I imagined I would have to stay in the building after school ended, that I would have to spend the night in school.

QUEENS WAS A port of entry for Indians. Indian stores were not specialized then. The same store that sold Red Fort rice also carried saris, also had calculators, blood pressure cuffs, and the sorts of things that people took back to India as gifts. Back then, even in Queens, there were not yet enough Indians for the stores to carry produce. To get bitter gourds and papayas and anything that might spoil, my father went to Chinatown.

In India, to earn blessings, my mother used to prepare extra rotis at every meal to feed the cows that wandered our neighborhood. In America, we went to temple on Fridays to, as my mother said, begin the weekend with a clean mind. Our temple was one of just a few on the Eastern Seaboard. Until recently it had been a church. Inside the large, dim chamber there were idols along three walls and the air smelled of incense, like the incense in temples in India. In India, though, temples also smelled of flowers, of sweat from the crowds, of spoilage from the milk used to bathe the idols. Here, along with the smell of incense, there was only a faint odor of mildew. Because the temple smelled so simple, it seemed fake.

ONE NIGHT, SNOW drifted down from a night sky. I felt like I was in a book or TV show.

FOR ME, THE two best things about America were television and the library. Every Saturday night I watched *The Love Boat*. I looked at the women in their one-piece bathing suits and their high heels and imagined what it would be like when I was married. I decided that when I was married, I would be very serious, and my silence would lead to misunderstand-

ings between me and my wife. We would have a fight and
later make up and kiss. She would be wearing a blue swimsuit
as we kissed.

Before we came to America, I had never read a book just
to read it. When I began doing so, at first, whatever I read
seemed obviously a lie. If a book said a boy walked into a
room, I was aware that there was no boy and there was no
room. Still, I read so much that often I imagined myself
in the book. I imagined being Pinocchio, swallowed by a
whale. I wished to be inside a whale with a candle burning
on a wooden crate, as in an illustration I had seen. Van-
ishing into books, I felt held. While at school and walking
down the street, there seemed no end to the world, when I
read a book or watched *The Love Boat*, the world felt simple
and understandable.

Birju liked America much more than I did. In India, he
had not been popular. Here he made friends quickly. He was
in seventh grade and his English was better than mine. Also,
he was kinder than he used to be in India. In India there had
been such competition, so many people offering bribes for
their children to get slightly better grades, that he was always
on edge. Here doing well seemed as simple as studying.

One of the boys that Birju befriended was an Indian from
Trinidad. My mother and Birju talked about him often. My
mother wanted Birju to avoid him because the boy did not get
good grades. I think she also looked down on him because he
was not from India and so was seen as out of caste.

"He thinks a sanitation engineer is an engineer, Mommy," Birju said, sounding upset, as if his friend's misunderstanding hurt him. "I told him it was a garbage man."

My mother was boiling rice at the stove. Birju, I remember, was standing beside her in a tee shirt with brown and yellow horizontal stripes that made him look like a bumblebee.

"Why is that your problem? Why are you going around educating him?"

"He doesn't have good parents. His mother and father aren't married. Neither one of them went to college."

"He'll drag you down before you save him."

My school was on the way to Birju's, so Birju used to walk me there every morning. One morning I started crying and told him about the bullying. He suggested that I talk to the teacher. When I didn't, he told our parents. My father came to school with me. I had to stand at the front of the class and point at all the boys who had shoved me and threatened me. After this, the bullying stopped. I had been upset that Birju told our parents. I hadn't thought that what he suggested would make a difference. The fact that it did surprised me.

In India, Birju had collected stamps, and he would sit for hours and look at them. Now, he made model airplanes. He spent whole days at our kitchen table, his mouth open, one hand holding tweezers and the other a magnifying glass.

. . .

My MOTHER TOOK a job in a garment factory. The morning that she was to start, she came into the living room wearing jeans. I had never seen her wearing something formfitting before. Birju and I were sitting on one of the mattresses. "Your thighs are so big," Birju said, laughing.

My mother started screaming. "Die, murderer, die."

Birju laughed, and I joined him.

In India, when my father said we should do something, we wouldn't really start doing it till our mother had decided whether it made sense. In America, our parents were closer to equal importance. My father had all sorts of plans for us. Mostly these involved us assimilating. He made us watch the news every evening. This was incredibly boring. We didn't care that there were hostages in Iran or that there was a movie called *The Empire Strikes Back*. He also bought us tennis rackets and took us to Flushing Meadows Park. There he made us hit tennis balls because he believed that tennis was a sport for rich people. Both Birju and I wore white headbands.

My father was still irritable and suspicious as he had been in India, but he also had a certain confidence, like no matter what happened he would have done one thing that was uncontestably wonderful. "A green card is worth a million dollars," he repeatedly told us. My mother, despite working in a garment factory, was mostly the same as she had been in India. She had been enthusiastic there about trying new things, taking me and Birju to movies and restaurants, and she was the same in America. She took Birju and me for walks in grocery stores so that we could see things we had never seen before—canned hearts of palms, boxes of colorful cereals. My mother said that she wished she was a teacher but she did not feel diminished by her work. "Work is work," she said.

My relationship with Birju changed. In India, my mother used to come home around the same time we did. Now, Birju was expected to take care of me until she returned from work. He was supposed to boil frozen shelled corn for me and give me a glass of milk. He was supposed to sit with me and watch me do my homework as he did his. Till America, I had somehow not paid much attention to the fact that Birju was older than I was. I had thought that he was bigger, but not more mature. Now, I began to understand that Birju dealt with more complicated things than I did.

BIRJU AND I were sent to spend the summer with our father's older sister. This was in Arlington, Virginia. She and our uncle lived in a small white two story house beside a wide road. The houses in Arlington had yards. The hot humid air there smelled of earth and the newness of green plants.

Among the exotic things about Arlington was that the television networks were on different channels than in Queens. I turned nine while I was there.

In Arlington, Birju began studying for the test to get into the Bronx High School of Science. He had to study five hours a day. While I got to go out, Birju had to stay in the living room and work until he was done with his hours.

When we returned to Queens, Birju had to study three hours every weeknight and all day on weekends. Many nights I fell asleep on my mattress as he sat at the round, white kitchen table, his pencil scratching away.

Despite all the time Birju was spending with his books, my mother felt that he was not studying hard enough. Often they fought. Once she caught him asleep on the foam mattress in the room that my parents shared. He had claimed that he needed quiet and so instead of studying at the kitchen table where he could be watched, he should be allowed to go into their room to study. When my mother came into the room, he was rolled onto his side breathing deeply.

She began shouting, calling him a liar. Birju ran past her into the kitchen and returned with a knife. Standing before her, holding the knife by the handle and pointing it at his stomach, he said, "Kill me. Go ahead; kill me. I know that's what you want."

"Do some work instead of being dramatic," my mother said contemptuously.

I became infected with the anxiety that Birju and my parents appeared to feel. When the sun shone and I went to Flushing Meadows Park, I had the sense that I was frittering away time. Real life was occurring back in our apartment with Birju studying.

The day of the exam finally came. On the subway to the test, I sat and Birju stood in front of me. I held one of his test preparation books in my lap and checked his vocabulary. Most of the words I asked him he didn't know. I started to panic. Birju, I began to see, was not going to do well. As I asked my questions and our mother and father watched, my voice grew quieter and quieter. I asked Birju what "rapscallion" meant. He guessed it was a type of onion. When I told him what it was, he began blinking quickly.

"Keep a calm head," my father scolded.

"Don't worry, baby," my mother said. "You will remember when you need to."

The exam took place in a large, white cinder block building that was a school but looked like a parking garage. The test started in the morning, and as it was going on, my parents and I walked back and forth nearby along a chain-link fence that surrounded basketball courts. The day was cold, gray, damp. Periodically, it drizzled. There were parked cars along the sidewalk with waiting parents inside, and the windows of these grew foggy as we walked.

My father said, "These tests are for white people. How are we supposed to know what 'pew' means?"

"Don't give me a headache," my mother said. "I'm worried enough."

"Maybe he'll do well enough in the math and science portions that it will make up for the English."

My stomach hurt. My chest was heavy. I had wanted the day of Birju's test to come so that it would be over. Now, though, that the day was here, I wished Birju had had more time.

Midway through the exam, there was a break. Birju came out on the sidewalk. His face looked tired. We surrounded him and began feeding him oranges and almonds—oranges to cool him and almonds to give his brain strength.

My mother was wearing Birju's backpack. "It's raining, baby," my mother said, "which means that it's a lucky day."

"Just do your best," my father said. "It's too late for anything else."

Birju turned around and walked back toward the building.

Weeks went by. It was strange for Birju not to be studying. It was strange not to see his study guides on the living room floor beside his mattress. It was as if something was missing and wrong. Often Birju wept and said, "Mommy, I know I didn't pass."

A month went by and then two. A warm day came when I could tie my winter coat around my waist during lunch hour, then another such day, like birds out of season. Spring came. In Delhi, they would be turning on fountains in the evening, and crowds would gather to watch.

The results arrived. Because Birju had said it so many

times, I knew that an acceptance letter would come in a thick envelope. The one that he showed me was thin and white. Tears slid down his cheeks.

"Maybe you got in," I murmured, trying to be comforting.

"Why do you think that?" Birju asked. He stared at me as if I might know something he did not.

Our mother was at work. She had said not to open the envelope until she arrived, that we would take it to temple and open it there. This made no sense to me. I thought what the envelope contained had already been decided.

My father arrived home after my mother. As soon as he did, Birju demanded that we go to temple.

Inside the large chamber, my mother put a dollar in the wooden box before God Shivaji. Then we went to each of the other idols in turn. Normally we only pressed our hands together before each idol and bowed our heads. This time we knelt and did a full prayer. After we had prayed before all the idols, we got on our knees before the family of God Ram. Birju was between our parents.

"You open it, Mommy."

My mother tore off one side of the envelope and shook out a sheet of paper. In the first paragraph was the answer: Yes!

"See? I told you we should open it at temple," she said.

We leapt to our feet and hugged.

With her arms still around Birju, my mother looked over his shoulder at me. "Tomorrow, we start preparing you," she said.

It sounded like a threat.

We began being invited to people's houses for lunch, for dinner, for tea. This was so Birju could be introduced to these people's children. Back then, because immigrants tended to be young and the Indian immigration to America had only recently begun, there were few Indians who could serve as role models.

We took the subway all over Queens, the Bronx. We even went into Manhattan. We traveled almost every weekend. My mother would sit quietly in people's living rooms and look on proudly as Birju talked.

Once, as we were getting ready to leave our apartment to go on one of these visits, Birju said, "Why do we have to go?"

My mother answered, "They have a girl they want you to marry." She said this and laughed.

"For me," my father said, "there is one thing only." He rubbed his thumb and forefinger together. "Dowry."

"Leave me alone," Birju said.

My father grabbed Birju and kissed his cheek. "Give me one egg, chicken. One egg only."

"Don't say that," my mother said. "We're vegetarian. Say, 'Give me some milk, goat, clean, pretty goat.'"

The pride of getting into his school changed Birju. He sauntered. Entering a room, he appeared to be leaning back. When we spoke, he would look at me as if he were looking at someone bafflingly stupid. One time when he looked at me this way, I blurted, "You have bad breath." I felt foolish for having pitied him when he was studying.

My mother acted as if everything Birju said was smart. One afternoon, as he sat leaning back in a chair at the kitchen table, only two of the chair's legs on the floor and one skinny arm reaching behind him and touching the wall so that he would not fall, he told our mother, "You should be a tollbooth collector."

"Why?" she asked from the stove, where she was boiling frozen corn.

"In a tollbooth, people will only see your top."

My mother had been talking about trying to get a government job. She didn't want to wear uniforms, though, because her hips embarrassed her.

She laughed and turned to me. "Your brother is a genius."

I wished I had thought of what Birju had said.

I wondered sometimes if my parents loved my brother more than they loved me. I didn't think so. They bothered him and corrected him so much more than they corrected me that I assumed they secretly preferred me to him.

Birju got a girlfriend. The girl was Korean. She had creamy white skin and a mole on her left cheek. She would visit while our parents were at work. I didn't like Birju having a girlfriend. A part of me thought that to be with a different race was unnatural, disgusting. Also, when she came over and they went into our parents' room and closed the door, I could see that Birju would one day be leaving our family, that one day he would have a life that had nothing to do with us. And since he would be going to the Bronx High School of Science and was the most valuable person in the family, this made me angry.

When Nancy was visiting, I would sometimes get upset. I would go knock on my parents' door and when Birju opened it, I would say he needed to give me milk.

After Nancy left, Birju used to hum, move around the apartment excitedly, periodically bursting into song. I once asked him what he and Nancy did behind the closed door. He said, "Babies like you don't need to know such things."

We went to Arlington again in the summer. By now, after almost two years in America, I had grown chubby. I could grip my stomach and squeeze it. Birju was tall and thin. He was five feet six and taller than our parents. He had a little mustache and tendrils of hair on the sides of his cheeks.

Once more I lay on my aunt's sofa and watched TV. Once more the TV shows in the afternoon were different from the ones in Queens, and they made me feel that I was living far from home. Once more I saw the lawns outside the houses of

Arlington, and it seemed to me that the people who lived in these houses must be richer, happier, and more like those on TV than my family or our neighbors in Queens.

Most days, Birju went to a swimming pool at a nearby apartment building. One afternoon in August, I was stretched out on my aunt's sofa watching *Gilligan's Island* when the telephone rang. The shades were drawn, making the room dim. After she hung up, my aunt came to the doorway. "Birju had an accident," she said. I didn't understand what she meant. "Get up." She motioned with a hand for me to rise. I didn't want to. *Gilligan's Island* was half over and by the time we got back from the pool where Birju was swimming, the show would be finished.

Outside, it was bright and hot. We walked along a sidewalk as cars whizzed by. There was a hot breeze. I kept my head down against the glare, but the light dazzled me.

The apartment building that had the pool was tall, brown, with its front covered in stucco and carved to resemble brick. The pool was to the side, surrounded by a chain-link fence. The building towered over it, like it felt disdain for the pool. There was a small parking lot next to the pool and an ambulance was parked there with a crowd of white people gathered by its rear.

We came up to the crowd. Being near so many whites made me nervous. Perhaps they would be angry with us for causing trouble. Birju should not have done whatever he had done.

My aunt said, "You wait," and moved forward. She had arthritis in one hip, and she pushed into the crowd with a lurching gait.

I remained at the edge of the crowd. Alone, I felt even more embarrassed. I couldn't see what was occurring. A minute passed and then two.

My aunt came back through the crowd. She was hobbling quickly.

"Go home," she said, her face strained. "I have to go to the hospital."

I started on my way back. I walked head down along the sidewalk. I was irritated. Birju had gotten into the Bronx High School of Science, and now he was going to get to be in a hospital. I was certain our mother would feel bad for him and give him a gift.

As I walked, I wondered whether Birju had stepped on a nail. I wondered if he was dead. This last was thrilling. If he was dead, I would get to be the only son.

The sun pressed heavily on me. Considering that Birju was going to a hospital, I decided I should probably cry.

I pictured myself alone in the house. I imagined Birju getting to be in the hospital while I had just another ordinary day. I imagined how next year Birju was going to get to be at the Bronx High School of Science and I would have to go to my regular school. Finally the tears came.

JUST AS I had expected, *Gilligan's Island* was over.

I lay back down on the sofa and watched TV until five,

when the news started. I then picked up a book and propped it on my stomach. I read for a while, but I was aware that my aunt was gone. I felt that something exciting was occurring and I was not getting to participate in an adventure.

Six o'clock. Usually around this time, my aunt would be in the kitchen, taking things out of the cabinets. The quietness of the kitchen felt eerie. I got up off the sofa, went out the back door, and stood on the wooden deck. There was my uncle's garden, the dusty tomato vines, the pepper plants with their hard, shiny green peppers.

I returned to the kitchen. The stillness and the empty counters struck me. Suddenly I felt like I had been forgotten, that nobody cared about me.

Around eight my uncle arrived in his dark pants and short-sleeve shirt, with his triangle of wispy white hair. He stood by the sink drinking a glass of water. He still had his shoes on. For him to be wearing shoes in the kitchen was so strange that it made the kitchen feel like it wasn't a real kitchen but a display in a furniture store.

"What's happened?" I asked.

He patted my head. "We don't know."

About ten thirty, my uncle drove us to the bus station. We were going to pick up my mother. The fact that my mother was coming made what had occurred seem very serious. When I breathed, I could feel my chest.

The bus station was a large, high chamber, with ceiling fans spinning far overhead. The air was heavy and warm and smelled of gasoline and salty french fries. Periodically there were loud announcements in which a man told us what bus had arrived or was about to leave. I sat on a wooden bench partitioned by wooden arms. A series of automatic doors kept flapping back and forth like the paddles of a pin-ball machine.

Finally, my mother walked through one of them. Her hair was loose, her face flattened with fear. She was wearing a yellow sari and carrying a black duffel bag.

Seeing my mother, I worried that she might think I was bad for not crying. I walked up to her. She looked down. It was as if she didn't recognize me. "Don't worry," I said. "I've cried already."

The hospital room was bright and white and noisy. There was the whir of machines and something beeping. There was a loud motorized rumble, almost like that of a generator.

Birju was lying on a bed with railings. The railings reminded me of a crib. There were poles on wheels all around the bed. The poles had bags hanging from them and also machines that were attached with clamps. Wires and tubes came from these and touched Birju. It was like he was in the middle of many clotheslines.

My mother stopped in the doorway. She started to cry. I stood beside her, holding the duffel bag before me. I became angry with Birju for having created this problem.

Birju had a plastic mask over his mouth and nose, making him look like a fighter pilot. His eyes were wide open, as if in panic. He appeared to be staring up at some invisible thing and that thing was pressing down on his chest.

Was the mask pumping a gas which was keeping him still? I imagined removing the mask, and Birju coughing and starting to speak. He would complain that people had not removed the mask earlier, that even I had known what to do.

BIRJU HAD DIVED into the swimming pool. He had struck his head on the pool's cement bottom and lain there stunned for three minutes. Water had surged down his throat, been dragged into his lungs as he tried to breathe. His lungs had peeled away from the insides of his chest.

Back at the house, my uncle carried a large cardboard box into the room that Birju and I had shared, and he placed it against a wall. My aunt and mother draped a white sheet over the box. They taped postcards of various gods on the wall so that these appeared to be gazing at the altar. On the altar itself, they placed a spoon and in the spoon, a wick soaked in clarified butter. They put a wad of dough on the altar and stuck incense sticks into the dough. They did all this quickly and quietly. When they spoke, it was in a whisper.

The ceiling lights were turned off. The flame in the spoon and the smoke rising from it sent shadows shaking over the walls. I lay down on a strip of foam beneath one of the windows. My aunt and mother stretched themselves face down before the altar. They sang prayers. "You can make a mute sing. You can make a cripple leap over a mountain." Their singing kept waking me. I understood that it was proper to pray in moments like these, but still, I knew that Birju was going to be all right—wouldn't it be better for everyone to get some sleep?

Around four in the morning, the ceiling lights were turned on. My first thought was that I had imagined everything.

But my mother was standing before the altar and the air was thick with incense. She had her hands pressed together and was wearing a blue silk sari and a gold necklace—she looked like she was going to a wedding. My aunt came into the room. She, too, was dressed as if for something special. She joined my mother in saluting the altar.

A little later, about to leave for the hospital, we stood in the driveway. It was still night. I looked up at the stars. There were thousands of them, some of them bright, some of them dim. I suddenly had the sense that what was happening was a mistake, that we had been given somebody else's life.

At the hospital, Birju's bed was empty. He had been taken for an operation. The four of us sat by the bed and sang prayers.

IN THE DAYS and weeks that followed, I spent most of each day sitting by Birju's bed chanting to him from the *Ramayana*. The book was a large hardcover wrapped in saffron cloth.

Some of the pages had grease stains from the butter used in prayers, and one could look through the stains and see the letters on the next page. Every time I opened the book, there was a puff of incense smell from the book having spent so many years near altars.

I had never prayed like this before, every day, hour after hour, praying till my throat became raw and even my tongue and gums hurt. I had not believed in God till then. Now, I started to think that people wouldn't be building temples, going on pilgrimages, if they weren't going to get something out of it. I began to believe there had to be a God, but that he was like the president, distant, busy, not interested in small things.

Time passed. One afternoon, I watched my mother cut Birju's fingernails. She looked scared as she did this. She had his hand forced open and was trying to keep it from clenching. "Is it all right?" she asked him. I felt like I was dreaming.

Birju had his oxygen mask removed. Many of the wheeled poles were taken away. Now with his eyes open he looked the way he always had except it was as if he was lost in thought. A doctor said Birju was blind, that oxygen deprivation had destroyed his corneas. It seemed disloyal to believe this; it seemed that the loyal thing was to believe that nothing much was wrong with him and that he would be better any day now. Hearing the doctor, I felt that I should be angry at him, that I should say God could do anything. I didn't feel anger, though. What I felt was pity for poor Birju. I wanted to kiss his cheeks. I wanted to tell him he was beautiful and that we would take care of him always.

Birju moaned, he yawned, he coughed, but even with his eyes open he appeared to be dreaming. Birju responded to things. If there was a loud noise, he turned his head in the direction of the sound. Then he rolled his head back and just lay there. Often he smacked his lips and puffed spit. Occasionally he had a seizure. His teeth would clamp shut and squeak against each other. His body would stiffen, his waist rise off the bed, and the bed would begin to rattle. Seeing this frightened me. I would stand by the bed and look at him through the railings and wonder what to do.

The accident had occurred in early August. September came and school began. I started attending school in Arlington. The school was three-quarters of a mile from my aunt and uncle's house.

I didn't cry at home or at the hospital because I didn't want to add to my parents' problems. On the way to school, though, I would. Strange things made me cry. The weight of my book bag, how it pushed me down would set me crying. Sometimes some thought of Birju would brush against me. My mother had written to the Bronx High School of Science and obtained a year's deferment. As I sobbed, I would be amazed at how much I loved my brother. I had not known he mattered so much to me.

At school, too, I wept. Sometimes when I felt the sobs starting, I looked down and held my breath and tried to think of other things—a television program, a book—but this wasn't always enough. My teacher would send me out into the schoolyard so that I didn't disturb the class.

The schoolyard had a swing set for little children and a slide. Otherwise, there was only a grassy field surrounded by a chain-link fence. I was embarrassed to be sent out. I felt foolish for behaving immaturely. I would walk along the fence and frequently I cried so hard that I lost my breath. When this happened, I became detached from myself. I walked and gasped and, as I did, I could feel my unhappiness walking beside me, waiting for my breath to return so that it could climb back inside me.

THE MOST IMPORTANT thing was to appeal to God. Each morning, my mother and I prayed before the altar. To me the altar was like a microphone—whatever we said in front of it would be broadcast directly to God. When I did my prayers, I traced an om, a crucifix, a Star of David onto the carpet by pressing against the pile. Beneath these I drew an S inside an upside-down triangle, for Superman. It seemed to me we should flatter anyone who could help.

One morning, I was doing my prayers before the altar when my mother came up to me. "What are you praying for?" she asked. She had her hat on, a thick gray knitted cap that had belonged to my uncle. The tracings on the carpet went against the weave and were darker than the surrounding nap. Pretending to examine them, I put my hand over the S. My mother did not mind the crucifix or the Star of David, but I knew she would be angry to catch me praying to a superhero, and in my nervousness I spoke the truth, "That God give me hundred percent on the math test."

My mother was silent for a moment. "What if God says you can have the math grade but Birju would have to be sick a little while longer?"

I looked at the altar. Kali Ma danced on a postcard, sticking out her tongue and waving her many swords and daggers. I knew my mother wanted to be angry. I saw that she wanted to complain. I thought of Birju in his hospital bed. I thought of how proud he used to be of dressing properly, tucking in his shirt so that it was snug around his waist, lacing and unlacing his shoes until the loops were as even as dragonfly wings, and of how nowadays he got rashes on his penis from the urinary catheter. I thought of these things, and it seemed OK that my mother should complain before the altar, where God was likely to hear and would take pity.

"Are you going to tell me about Kusum mausiji again?"

"Why not? When I was in tenth standard and your aunt was sick, I walked seven times around the temple and said, 'God, let me fail as long as you make Kusum better.'"

"If I failed the math test and told you that story, you'd slap me and say, 'What does one have to do with the other?'"

My mother turned toward the altar. "What sort of sons did you give me? One you nearly drown and the other is this fool."

I made my face earnest and looked at the altar so that God could see my sweetness. "I will fast today so that God puts some sense into me."

"No," my mother said. "You are a growing boy. Fasting is good for me. I gain blessings and lose weight at the same time."

IN THE MORNINGS I prayed, and at night, when I was supposed to be sleeping but couldn't, I spoke with God. One rainy night, the room was gray with light from the street and my mother was lying nearby, her breath whistling. I was on my strip of foam and I asked God whether he minded being prayed to only in need. "You think of your toe only when you stub it," he said.

"Still, it's better to pray just to pray."

"It's human nature. I don't mind it." God looked like Clark Kent. He was wearing a gray cardigan and slacks. He sat cross-legged at the foot of the mat. Originally, right after the accident when I had first started talking to him, God had looked like Krishna. But it had felt foolish to discuss brain damage with someone who was blue and was holding a flute and had a peacock feather in his hair.

"You're not angry with me for touching the tree?"

"No, I'm flexible."

There was a large oak tree on the way to school. It stood half on the sidewalk and half off it. Because the tree looked very old, I thought it might know God from when there were fewer things in the world. Usually as I passed it, I would touch the tree and bring my hand to my forehead the way I did when I had touched my grandfather's feet.

"I respect you. The tree is just a way of showing respect to my elders."

God laughed. "I am not too caught up in formalities."

I became quiet. I was convinced that I had been marked as special by Birju's accident. To me it appeared obvious that the beginnings of all heroes contained misfortune. Both God Krishna and Superman had been separated from their parents at birth. Batman, too, had been orphaned. God Ram had to spend fourteen years in the forest, and it was only then that he did things that made him famous. I waited until it would not seem improper to talk about myself.

"How famous will I be?" I finally asked.

"I can't tell you the future," God said.

"Why not?"

"Even if I told you something, I might change my mind."

"But it would be harder for you to change your mind after you have said something will happen."

God laughed again. "You'll be so famous that fame will be a problem."

I sighed and wiggled into the foam strip.

"I want Birju's accident to lead to something." Saying this felt noble.

"He won't be forgotten."

"I can't just be famous, though. I need money, too. I need to take care of Mommy and Daddy."

"First you grab the finger, and then you grab the wrist."

"I'm just being practical."

"Don't worry. You can hardly imagine the life ahead."

This last statement made me happy.

It seemed obvious that God was more likely to help people who were good than those who were ordinary. This is why it felt very important that we behaved impeccably. My parents refused to do this, however.

My father was strange as always. Right after the accident, when he had first visited Birju, he had stood by the hospital bed, his face swollen and dark, his voice choked, and said, "Don't think I don't blame you. Don't think I don't know this is all your fault. What was in the pool? What was in there that you had to jump before anybody else got to it? Was there gold? Was there treasure?"

Since then, he had continued to say embarrassing things. Recently he had said that perhaps Birju had dived into the pool because of all the comic books he read, that Birju had thought he might gain superpowers by doing something like this.

"Shut up," my mother had replied.

But my mother was not behaving well, either. She picked fights when she could have just been quiet.

Every Friday night my father arrived on a Greyhound bus. He left on Sunday evenings to go back to New York. All weekend my parents would fight.

One Saturday afternoon in October, a nurse's aide, a large black woman in a white uniform, came into Birju's room to replace his catheter. As she walked out, my father accompanied her to the door. "Thank you," he said in the doorway.

When he came back to the hospital bed, my mother glared at him. "Don't say, 'Thank you, thank you.' Don't say, 'You are so good. You are so kind.' If you do, they will think you're weak." Recently, the hospital had told us that Birju needed to be moved, that now that his condition was stable, he needed to be put in a nursing home. The problem was that the insurance company was saying it wouldn't pay for a nursing home and so over the last few weeks, my mother had been getting into screaming matches with the hospital administrators who wanted us to leave.

"That's how you think," my father said, flaring up. "To you everybody is an enemy. If I smile, I have committed a sin." It seemed obvious that my father felt caught and so was trying to distract from his mistake.

"If I weren't willing to fight," my mother shouted, "if I weren't willing to scream, they would put Birju on the street. They would say it is time to go and here is your bill and there is the door. The only reason they haven't forced Birju out is because they are frightened, because they don't want to fight with someone who's crazy."

"Yes, you are crazy. I have always said you're crazy."

"And you're a coward. You don't want to do the hard things. You want to flatter and be nice and hope that these nurses and doctors will do everything Birju needs on their own. They won't. They will do the ordinary things but not the hard things. For the hard things you have to fight. These doctors and nurses just want you to be silent. They don't care what happens as long as you don't cause trouble."

My parents fought, and I was becoming lazy. Now when I came to the hospital after school, I no longer wanted to sit by Birju's bed and sing prayers. Singing prayers bored me. Often when I got to his room, I would tell my mother that I had homework and would go to the children's lounge down the hall.

The lounge had blue walls and yellow bookcases with picture books. There was a yellow beanbag and a large television. I liked to sit on the beanbag before the TV with a book in my lap and read while the TV played. Whenever commercials started, I would look down at the book and read. I liked books where the hero was a young man, preferably under twenty-five, who had a magical power that he discovered over the course of the book. *Riddle of Stars*, *The Chronicles of Amber*, *A Wizard of Earthsea*—I read these over and over. Reading a book a second time was more comforting than reading it the first because during the second reading everything was in its place. I read and watched TV so much that sometimes when I closed my eyes, images flickered before me.

I felt that there was something bad about being lost in my imagination. Occasionally, there were fall days that were so beautiful that I thought I would never see a day so lovely again. I would think this and then go back to reading or watching TV.

One evening when I was in the lounge, I saw a rock star being interviewed on *Entertainment Tonight*. The musician, dressed in a sleeveless undershirt that revealed a swarm of tattoos on his arms and shoulders, looked past the interviewer and began shouting at the camera. "Don't watch me! Live your life! I'm not you." I was filled with a sudden desire. I hurried out of the lounge and went down the hall and left the hospital. I stood outside the main entrance.

Now that I was outside, I didn't know what to do. It was cold and dark and there was an enormous moon. Cars leaving the parking lot stopped one by one at the edge of the road. I watched as they waited for an opening in the traffic, their brake lights glowing.

"Are things getting worse?" I asked God. November had just begun. Soon it would be Thanksgiving and then Christmas, and after this there would be a new year and in that year there would not have been a single day in which Birju had walked or talked.

"What do you think?"

"They seem to be."

"At least Birju's hospital hasn't forced him out."

"At least Birju isn't dead. At least Daddy's bus has never fallen off a bridge."

God was silent.

"I'm ashamed," I said.

"About what?"

"That after the accident, I was glad I might become an only child."

"Everybody thinks strange thoughts," God said. "It doesn't matter if you think something."

"When I was walking around in the schoolyard and you asked if I would switch places with Birju, I thought, *No.*"

"That, too, is normal."

"Why don't you make Birju like he was?"

As soon as I asked the question, God stopped feeling real. I knew then that I was alone, lying under my blanket, my face exposed to the dark.

"Christ was my son. I loved Job. How long did Ram have to live in the forest?"

"What does that have to do with me?" Normally this was the time to start discussing my glorious future. But the idea of a future in which Birju was sick made fame seem pointless.

"I can't tell you what the connection is, but you'll be proud of yourself."

I didn't say anything. God and I were silent for a while.

"What are three minutes for you?" I asked. "Just get rid of the three minutes when Birju was at the bottom of the pool."

"Presidents die in less time than that. Planes crash in less time than that."

I opened my eyes. My mother was on her side, and she had a blanket pulled up to her neck. She looked like an ordinary woman, her face sagging, her mouth open. It surprised me that you couldn't tell, just by looking at her, that she spent all day every day in a hospital, that she spent all day sitting by her son who was in a hospital bed, who was once going to go to the Bronx High School of Science but who was now so brain damaged that he could not walk or talk, could not turn over in his sleep, and had to be fed through a rubber tube that went into his side.

AND I KNEW things were getting worse. My parents fought with such anger that it was as if they hated each other.

One fall day, when all the trees had lost their leaves and the world looked like a fire had gone through it, my parents fought so bitterly in Birju's room that my mother told my father to go home and take me with him. My father drove us away. The route back to my aunt's took us along unpopulated two-lane roads. There were scrubby trees along the road, and between them I could see a lowering misty sun chasing us.

On one of the roads was a small bar with a gravel lot. The bar looked as if it had been a house once. Now it had a neon

sign, an orange hand lifting a sudsy mug of beer. Instead of
driving past, my father turned into the lot. I wondered why.
I had never known anyone who drank. I had always assumed
that people who drank were either Muslims or poets, or else
rich and depraved.

The tires made a crunching sound as we rolled up toward the
wooden steps of the little house. "One minute," my father said,
and reached past me and pushed open the door on my side.

Inside, the bar was dark and the air smelled of cigarette smoke
and something stale and sweet. The floor was linoleum, like the
kitchen at my aunt's. A basketball game was playing on the TV.

My father spoke to the bartender, a big man in a sleeveless
sweatshirt. "Is anything half off?"

"Well drinks."

"I'll have a double of your cheapest whiskey."

My father lifted me onto a stool. I looked around. There
was an old, fat man in shorts sitting at a table. He was wearing
an undershirt, and his stomach sat in his lap like a small child.
He was wearing sneakers and no socks and the skin around
his ankles was black like a bruised banana.

The bartender returned with the drink. My father drank it
in a gulp. It was the first glamorous thing I had ever seen him
do. It was the act of a gangster or cowboy. Then he ordered
another. The announcer raised his voice, and we looked at the
TV. My father asked if I had ever seen a basketball game all
the way through.

"I've seen the Harlem Globetrotters."

"I've heard they don't play other teams because they can defeat everyone else so easily."

"They only play against each other or if the president asks, like when they had to play against aliens to save the earth."

"Aliens?"

I realized that my father had been teasing me and I had confused TV with reality. My ears became hot.

The second drink came. My father drank this quickly, too, and asked for a beer. As we waited, he put his elbows on the bar. "I never thought this would be my life," he said.

The sun was setting when we left the bar. The air was moist and cold. In the car, my father rolled down his window.

AROUND THANKSGIVING, THE insurance company said that it would pay for a nursing home. No one was happier to hear this than my aunt. "There is no point in denying what has happened, Shuba. We have to keep trusting God. We can't just trust God when he's doing what we want. We have to trust him even when things are not as we would like them."

In December, my aunt's only grandson turned one. She had a birthday party for him and didn't tell us. When we came home from the hospital the night of the party and saw people sitting in the living room eating cake from paper plates, my aunt led us back into the kitchen. She said, "I thought it would depress you, seeing other people's happiness."

"Are you other people?" my mother said. "Is your happiness not my happiness?"

"Have some cake," she said. "What is there to be angry about? I made a mistake." As my aunt walked out of the kitchen, she said, loud enough to be heard by the guests, "I feel like I'm in court. Every word I have to watch."

Two weeks later, my mother told me that we were moving to a new home in New Jersey.

As CHRISTMAS DREW near, a Christmas tree appeared in the hospital's lobby, and the hallways began to have cutouts of Santa on his sleigh taped to the walls. I began praying whenever I thought of it—at my locker, during lunch, even in the middle of a quiz. I prayed more than I had ever prayed before, but I found it harder and harder to drift into the rhythm of sung prayers or into the nightly conversations with God. How could chanting and burning incense undo three minutes of a sunny August afternoon? It was like trying to move a sheet of blank paper from one end of a table to the other by blinking so fast that you started a breeze.

On Christmas Eve, my mother asked the hospital chaplain to come to Birju's room and pray. She and I knelt with the priest beside Birju's bed. Afterward, the chaplain asked my mother whether she would be attending Christmas services the next morning. "Of course, Father," she said.

"I'm coming, too," I said.

That night, I watched *It's a Wonderful Life* on television in the living room. To me, the movie meant that if you become unhappy enough, almost anything can pass as happiness. Later, when I lay down near my parents and closed my eyes, God appeared.

A part of me felt that God would have to grant whatever request was made of him on his son's birthday. "Will Birju be better in the morning?"

"No," God answered.

"Why not?"

"When you asked for the hundred percent on the math test, you could have asked for your brother."

The next morning, when I arrived at the hospital with my mother and father, Birju was asleep, breathing through his mouth while a nurse's aide stood by the hospital bed, pouring a can of Isocal formula into his G-tube, the yellowish rubber hose that went into his stomach. I hadn't expected Birju to be better; still, seeing him this way made my chest very heavy.

All day, I sat in a corner of Birju's room. My mother sat by the hospital bed and read women's magazines to Birju while she shelled peanuts into her lap. My father was reading a thick red book in preparation for a civil-service exam. The day wore on. The sky outside grew dark. At some point, the lights were turned on, and at the idea of the day being over and nothing having changed, I started crying. I tried to be quiet. I did not want my parents to notice my tears and think that I was crying for Birju, because in reality I was crying for myself, for having to spend so much time in the hospital, for now having to move to a town I didn't know.

My father noticed first. "What's the matter, hero?"

My mother shouted, "What happened?" She jumped up. She looked so alarmed that it was as if I were bleeding.

"I didn't get any Christmas presents. I need a Christmas present," I said. "You didn't buy me a Christmas present." And then, because I had revealed my selfishness, I let myself weep. "You have to give me something. I should get something for all this." I clenched my hands and wiped my face with my fists. "Each time I come here, I should get something."

My mother pulled me up and pressed me into her stomach. My father came and stood beside us. "What do you want?" he said.

I didn't know.

"What do you want?" my mother repeated.

"I want to eat pizza, and I want candy."

My mother stroked my hair. "Don't worry, baby."

I sobbed, and she kept wiping my face with a fold of her sari. At last I stopped crying, and she and my father decided that I should be taken back to my aunt's.

On the way, we stopped at a strip mall. It was a little after five, and the streetlights were lit. First, my father and I went to a magazine shop and bought a bag of 3 Musketeers bars and a bag of Reese's Peanut Butter Cups. Then we went next door to a pizza shop. We sat in a booth and kept our coats on as we ate. Since the accident, I had said a quick prayer whenever I ate. Now I wondered whether to pray. It seemed that I should still do everything possible to help Birju. I brought my hands together over the paper plate.

Later, in the car, I held the bags of candy in my lap while my father drove in silence. Even through the plastic, I could smell the sugar and chocolate. Some of the houses we passed were dark. Others were outlined in Christmas lights.

The car was warm and after a while, I rolled down the window slightly. The car filled with roaring wind. We approached the apartment building with the pool where Birju had had his accident. Because of the lights in the parking lot where the ambulance had stood, I could see the tall fence that guarded the pool. I tried to see past the fence into the dark beyond. I wondered what had happened to the pool's unlucky water after the accident. Had it been drained? Probably it had not. All summer long, people must have swum in the pool and sat on its sides, splashing their feet in the water, and not known that my brother had lain for three minutes on its concrete bottom one August afternoon.

We stood in my aunt's driveway with our luggage in the car. "What has happened?" she sobbed. "What has God done?" As she and my mother hugged, my aunt clutched at her and would not let go. My mother gripped my aunt too and wept. My uncle was there. He put a hand on my shoulder, and I wanted to shrug it off. I was shivering, and my coat was in the car. Why hadn't people been nicer when it mattered? I wondered.

ON MY FIRST day in the nursing home, I sat by Birju's bed and read to him from an old issue of *Chandamama*. It was raining and drops clicked off the windows. The room was about the size of the one in the hospital. Even with the ceiling lights on, it was dim. My mother kept walking in and out of the room. She was busy doing paperwork. When she entered, I continued reading without looking up. I had the

sense that I was being watched, that we were providing evidence to the nursing home. I needed to show that my family
was admirable and that we cared about Birju. I felt that if I
did this, it would shame the people at the home to take good
care of my brother.

I began to ache from sitting on the hard chair. My voice
got hoarse. At the hospital, I would have said, "Birju, let's
watch some TV." More hours passed. I was conscious of how
quiet the nursing home was. The door behind me was open.
When a cart went by, I could hear its wheels hissing along
the linoleum. At the hospital, there were always nurses and
doctors hurrying about. The PA system regularly came on.
The quietness made me feel that the home was not as good
as the hospital, that the nursing home was where the world
put people who were not important, people who could be
put away someplace and forgotten. I began to feel that we
had let Birju down, that by letting him be moved here, we
had not taken care of him.

The nursing home stood on one side of a road and opposite
it was a hospital. The two were connected by a bridge that
looked like a plastic straw. At five o'clock, my mother and I
lifted Birju from his bed. My mother slipped her arms through
his underarms, and I held him around the knees. We swung
him into a wheelchair and rolled him through the hallways
onto the bridge. There, facing out, our image reflected back at
us, we waited for my father to come from the train station. He
worked in New York, and each morning he took a train into

the city. That evening, when my father arrived, he said that he had seen us hovering above the road, snow falling past us.

That first day, he wasn't drunk. But almost every day after this, he was. Sometimes he would smell of beer and other times of scotch. "Another bastard day," he would say bitterly in Birju's room.

In the beginning, my mother remained silent about my father's drinking. She looked shocked. I could tell she wasn't speaking because she didn't want to say anything in front of me. I knew that this meant I, too, was supposed to pretend not to see, and yet I wasn't sure whether this meant I should act busy and energetic so that it would appear that I was too frantic to be able to see anything or whether I should act as I always had.

Later, after perhaps ten days, my mother began to acknowledge that my father was drinking. First she was sarcastic. She muttered under her breath. "You are going to kill someone driving this way." My father ignored her.

Then she became openly angry. Wet-eyed, she shouted at him. "You have a son like this, and what do you do? Drown yourself."

My parents had moved to Metuchen because it was one of the few towns in New Jersey that had a temple. A month or so after we arrived, my mother combed my hair and took me with her to see the pundit. It was a Tuesday night, one of three evenings when he sat at the temple, another converted church with the musty American smell and a large idol-lined chamber with a refrigerator in the back for the ceremonial milk and bananas.

My mother explained our situation to the pundit. "Birju is in a coma," she said, though Birju's eyes were open and he was not in a coma, but was brain damaged. "The doctors say that they don't know what can happen. He could wake tomorrow." I wondered why she was saying this. I guessed that it must be because people are more likely to help if they think there is hope. If there isn't any, they might try to avoid us, because who wants to be around someone depressing? "I go every morning to the nursing home. His father comes in the evening. I am so glad there is a temple in town."

The pundit stood before us, leaning slightly forward. He was a handsome man in his thirties, tall, broad shouldered, with a thick mustache. It was strange to come to a pundit for help. This was not what one would have done in India. In India, pundits are not counselors or spiritual leaders, but functionaries, performers of rituals, the equivalent of low level government clerks who put stamps on papers and who always have their hands out for a bribe. My mother used to speak of pundits with disgust. "Nobody has ever seen the back of a pundit's hands," she would say. Once, she told a joke about a pundit who fell into a deep hole. People reached down into it and said, "Give us your hand." When they said this, the pundit crossed his arms and began pouting. An old man then pushed his way to the front of the crowd. He said, "Is this any way to talk to a pundit?" He reached into the hole and said, "Take my hand." Immediately, the pundit grabbed it.

I felt contempt for the pundit because he was a pundit. I also felt contempt for him because he was not a real one. Mr. Narayan was an engineer who volunteered at the temple. In the seventies through the mideighties, when most of us prayed in one another's homes, even communities that had managed to buy or build a temple could not afford to pay a pundit, and so the pundits tended to be volunteers, usually especially pious men who, because of their piety and because of a reputation for virtue, were asked if they would be willing to lead ceremonies and sit in the temple on certain nights. In India, it was unheard of for a pundit to visit parishioners who were sick, or to offer help to families in trouble. These volunteer pundits, though, perhaps because they were just very decent people, behaved like the Christian pastors in the hospital.

A few days later, Mr. Narayan came to visit us in Birju's room. It was a cold and sunny Saturday afternoon. It had been important to get him to come during the day so that my father would not be drunk. Mr. Narayan sat in a chair along the side of the hospital bed. He did not seem to care that Birju had his eyes open and so was not in a coma—perhaps the word coma did not mean something specific to him? Mr. Narayan sat up straight with his hands in his lap. It was strange to have him there. I had grown so used to our being alone with Birju that I had begun to feel that my brother was no longer real to the outside world. Yet Mr. Narayan's presence made Birju feel less important—the fact that seeing Birju did not cause everything to change for Mr. Narayan made it seem like what had happened was not as important as I thought it was.

Mr. Narayan had a bright, modest smile. He appeared eager to please and nodded at everything my parents said. His friendliness irritated me. "Why should I be proud of what I am doing?" my father said. "I am not glad to be doing it. I hate doing it." Mr. Narayan nodded, as if this frankness showed virtue and he was agreeing not with the statement but with the honesty.

My mother, who was standing behind my father's chair, would not let him say this unchallenged. "Whatever you say, I am happy I'm here to take care of my son. What if I were dead and there was nobody to care for Birju? Thank God I have breath in me so I can love him."

The pundit had us invited to a Ramayan Path in somebody's house. The steps leading up to the front door were covered in slippers and sandals and sneakers. Inside, too, the foyer was swimming in shoes and sandals. To our left was the living room. It was empty of furniture. White sheets were spread over the floor, and a man sat near the altar at the front and read from a *Ramayana* in his lap.

It had been a long time since we were around so many people.

"What are we going to do?" my father murmured, looking down as he stepped on the back of his loafers to pop them off.

"We're going to meet people," my mother hissed.

We went into the room to our right. This was jammed with guests and also sofas standing on their ends. There were so many people that I could only mostly see stomachs and waists. Walking through the crowd, nervous, I felt that the men and women around me were not living real lives, that my family, because it was suffering so intensely, was living a life that was more real than these people's, whose lives were silly like a TV show.

My mother and I and my father ended up in the kitchen. Here the light was diffuse because of the steam from the pots boiling on the stove. Our hostess, a large Punjabi woman, came up to us. She had a ponytail and was wearing the baggy shirt and pantaloons of a *salwar kameez*.

"Ah, Mrs. Mishra," she said, taking my mother's small hands in her large ones, "your story is like a fairy tale."

I liked this flattery. Still, I felt that our torment was being diminished by being compared to something unreal.

"Brother-in-law, thank you for coming. When I tell people your story, they are amazed." Mrs. Kohli pressed her hands together before her. My father stammered a *namaste*.

Mrs. Kohli introduced us to a woman standing nearby. The woman was in pants and a shiny silk blouse. This meant either that she was lower class, since she was not dressed appropriately for a religious ceremony, or she was very educated and did not have to be like other people. "Her son is in a nursing home," Mrs. Kohli told the woman.

"My son had an accident in a swimming pool," my mother said. "He's in a coma." She said this shyly, as if she were sharing something precious. I became irritated. I thought, *No. Birju is not in a coma. He is brain damaged. He is destroyed.*

"Can he not talk at all?" the woman asked.

"No," my mother said and looked embarrassed.

"If you are in a room with him and sitting next to him, will he not know it?"

"There is no coma," my father said. "He is not asleep. Our son has his eyes open. He can't walk or talk. My wife says this coma thing because she thinks this sounds better."

Mrs. Kohli smiled. She nodded her head proudly. "See? A parent's love knows no shore."

My father said, "I'm going to go sit down."

Mrs. Kohli took us to meet other women. Again, my mother said that Birju was in a coma. These women, too, kept asking whether Birju really could not talk at all.

About an hour or so after we arrived, the reading of the *Ramayana* was nearing its end. Women sat cross-legged with their heads covered as if they were in temple. My mother and I sat together. My father sat nearby, his head bowed, looking down at the white sheet.

Usually, the host or hostess is the one who reads the end of the *Ramayana*. Mrs. Kohli came walking through the crowd, stepping carefully past knees. She reached my mother and me. Looking at my mother, she said, "Please come. Read the last verses."

"Ji, that is for you to do." My mother appeared at a loss, like someone trying to refuse an expensive gift from someone she hardly knew.

WE BEGAN RECEIVING invitations to people's houses, usually in connection with some religious ceremony. When we went, we were treated very respectfully, especially my mother. As soon as she entered a house, she was surrounded by women. It was as if we represented something—love of family, sacrificing for others. I, too, began to say that Birju was in a coma. This seemed what people wanted to hear. Once I told a man that Birju was brain damaged, that there was no hope, and he looked down at me and smiled and nodded like I was saying something other than what I actually was.

People visited us at the nursing home. Mostly these were couples with children. Often, it appeared, they hoped to teach their children a lesson. Once a man scolded his five-year-old daughter in front of us, "See what we do for you? Would an American do what Auntie and Uncle are doing? An American would say, 'You have to stand on your own two feet. You live your life, and I will live mine.' This is what we Indians do. We love our children too much. Go touch Birju brother's feet." The girl went slowly, hesitantly, to the hospital bed. Birju was wearing white socks. His feet were lying on a sheepskin, and because their tendons had shrunk, they turned inwards and almost met.

We also had men visit who said they could make Birju normal. These were men who worked as travel agents, candy-shop owners, engineers. A few came with their wives. Most came alone. Once, a mathematician who taught at a university visited. He had a horseshoe of hair around his scalp and a little narrow mustache. He sat by Birju with his hands on his stomach, his legs stretched before him, and he began quietly to lecture on Hindu scripture. He chuckled as he spoke, as if he were surprised by his own intelligence. Some of the words he used were English, and he used these when he wanted to show that he recognized science. "Ji, this *akashvani*, obviously this is a radio." He said "obviously" in English. "Many things," he said in English, "which Westerners say they invented, we had thousands of years ago. Aeroplanes. Television." Then he switched to Hindi. "There is proof. It is not like I am just saying this." He said this and laughed. He picked his nose, examined the snot, and flicked it beneath Birju's bed.

I was used to people saying Indians had invented most things. I had heard such claims many times before. A few men that visited said God had appeared to them in a dream and told them how to wake Birju. Others said that they had learned a cure from a saint in India.

I did not like these "miracle workers." It seemed to me

that they wanted to try their so-called cures on Birju because doing so would make them feel that they were at the center of important things. Still, there was comfort in having visitors. I dreaded the moment of their departure, when my parents and I would be alone again with Birju. When people left, the loneliness came so quickly that it was as if a window had been opened and cold air had rushed in. Sometimes this loneliness was so great that I almost wished that they had not visited.

Ordinary people, people who were calm, cheerful, and polite, also came. They invited us to their homes for dinner. In some ways my mother liked them more. With her suspicious nature, she saw melodrama as a way of covering things up. But the melodramatic people said more extreme things. They gave us more attention.

EVERY DAY AT two-thirty, my mother would fetch me from school and bring me to the nursing home. My father arrived at six. At seven, we went back to our apartment.

Our apartment consisted of one room with a sofa in the middle, facing a kitchenette and a television that sat on a cardboard box. Each night, I flung a sheet over the sofa and slept on it. My parents slept on a sponge mattress behind the sofa. On Friday and Saturday nights, my father stayed up very late watching movies on the VCR. Before the accident, he hadn't liked movies as much as my mother and I did. Now, he sat right in front of the television with the sound turned very low until two or three in the morning. He liked comedies especially: *Gol Maal, Naram Garam, Chhoti Si Baat.* Periodically through the night, I would wake and the room would be jumping with blue lights. When I rolled over on my side, I would see my father sitting there, directly in front of the TV. Almost always, he was drunk. His mouth would be open as if he were captivated by what he was seeing. Sometimes on weekends, my father did not come to the nursing home until noon or one o'clock. He would remain lying on the mattress as we ate breakfast. He would remain lying there as my mother and I left and stepped into the hallway.

Spring came. In the park that we passed on our way to and from the nursing home, the branches of the trees grew mossy with budding leaves. And then summer arrived. School ended, and I spent all day at the home.

In the morning, when we left the apartment, it would be bright and hot and humid. Our building was near the end of Main Street, a few hundred yards from the large old post office. There were parking meters on the sidewalk, gray metal poles the shape of matchsticks, upright, proper, brave, waiting for a coin so that they could come to life. When I walked past a parking meter, I would reach out and touch it.

We had sued the apartment building where Birju had had his accident. There had been a lifeguard on duty as Birju lay underwater. The fact that Birju was not spotted quickly was one mistake. When he was dragged out and was lying by the side of the pool, he was not given mouth-to-mouth resuscitation. This was a second mistake.

My father said that Birju had not gotten mouth-to-mouth resuscitation because he was Indian.

"Shut up," my mother shouted.

This was in Birju's room. My father was drunk, but he had said the same thing sober many times during the months that we waited for the financial settlement. I knew that what my father was saying was a lie. Hearing him say this was comforting, though, because then Birju's accident was no longer purely accidental, unconnected to the larger world, lacking all meaning. Also, there was something satisfying about being angry.

. . .

A YEAR HAD GONE by since Birju's accident. My father
began shaving him. The first time he did this was one afternoon. My mother and I stood and watched as he put shaving
cream on Birju's cheeks. "Take your time," my mother said.
"Be careful."

Birju lay there calmly as my father lathered him. It seemed
unfair that something like this could happen and the world
go on.

One Friday night in December, my father came home late.
My mother was cooking dinner. He entered the apartment
and leaned back against the gray metal door. He was smiling.
He crossed a foot over a knee and began unlacing a boot.

"Do you have news?" my mother asked.

"Yes," my father said. He kept smiling.

"Don't say anything."

My mother took a spoon, dug it into the sugar bowl that was
on the counter, and passed it to him. My father put the heaped
spoon in his mouth. The handle stuck out like a thermometer.

My mother said, "Now you can speak."

My father removed the spoon. "Six hundred and eighteen
thousand dollars."

I didn't know what this meant. I had thought we might get
a hundred million dollars or maybe a billion. Six hundred and
eighteen thousand dollars was so small that it hardly seemed
to count. It seemed a very ordinary thing, like a cup or a pair
of shoes.

I began to feel I had not heard correctly. I was lying on the sofa, a hardcover science fiction book standing upright on my stomach.

My mother stared at my father. She was yellowy in the apartment's fluorescent light, and the skin beneath her eyes looked singed. "You said it would be one million."

"A third goes to the lawyer."

"That means six hundred and sixty-six thousand."

"There were expenses."

"Fifty thousand dollars to mail letters, to xerox," she said angrily.

"Shuba, Shuba."

"What did he do for three hundred thousand dollars?" My mother said this and looked away from my father. She was silent. After a moment, she turned back to him. "I don't care about money. As long as we can afford medicine, that's all that matters."

She spread newspaper on the floor, and we sat down to eat. My mouth was dry as I chewed, and when I swallowed, the roti felt sharp.

After dinner we walked to the temple to give thanks. It was snowing. The snowflakes, as they drifted through the glow of the streetlights, resembled moths. I thought about the amount of the settlement.

My father had said that financial settlements were based on how much the person injured could earn. As I walked, I thought of how much the money meant in terms of hourly pay.

I reasoned that my mother went to the nursing home every day. She was there from eight thirty to seven. This meant she worked about ten hours a day, seven days a week. I was there from three to seven every weekday and both days on the weekend. I was not working all the time, though, when I was at the home. My father was also there on weeknights and weekends. If I were to undercount, my father and I each spent twenty hours a week at the nursing home. Birju was damaged all the time, and so this could count as a hundred hours of work a week. Two hundred and ten hours a week times fifty weeks was about ten thousand hours a year. If Birju remained alive for ten years, that was a hundred thousand hours of work. Six hundred and eighteen divided by a hundred was six dollars and eighteen cents.

I had been hoping for a ridiculously low sum, like a dollar. When I got the six dollars and eighteen cents, I was startled. My mother, I knew, had gotten paid five and a half dollars an hour when she worked at the sewing factory. Six dollars and eighteen cents did not seem unfair for a boy.

The next day in Birju's room, my mother proposed that my father take me to a movie. It was as if we had decided to pretend that we had received good news and should celebrate. My mother said I should see *Gandhi*. "Go see it and learn something." I didn't want to see a movie. I felt shame at the thought of spending money. If I were going to see a movie, though, I wanted to see *E.T.* "What rubbish," my mother said. "Monsters from the moon."

• • •

THE AGREEMENT CAME in the mail. It was actually several contracts printed on legal-sized paper. Because we didn't have a table in our apartment, my father spread the contracts on the sofa. He and my mother kneeled and signed. I wondered if I, too, would be asked to sign. I hadn't signed many things in my life. I imagined refusing and demanding more money. I asked my mother if I had to sign.

She laughed. She kissed me. "Why should you sign?"

It seemed to me that the judge who had decided how much Birju was worth must have also decided that I didn't matter very much. I might talk about loving my brother, but he probably hadn't believed that I actually did.

THE NURSING HOME that Birju was in was not good. We had known this for a while. One morning my mother and I walked into Birju's room. The lights were off and the window shades down. Birju was on his bed, on his side, behind the raised railings. He was panting.

My mother turned on the lights. Tears were streaming down Birju's face. He was propped up by pillows. Every two hours an aide was supposed to enter Birju's room and turn him from one side to the other. The night aide must have forgotten to do so.

"Every night when I leave him, I feel like I'm leaving him

in a stairwell," my mother said. She hurried around the bed so that she was between the bed and the wall. She told me to come hold Birju so that he remained on his side. I put my hands on his arm and hip. He was so wet from sweat it was as if someone had poured water over him. My mother removed the pillows, and I slowly lowered my brother onto his back.

Regularly, we found things lying beneath Birju, things that the night aides had dropped: thermometers, latex gloves, cookies, once even a pair of scissors. What scared us most was when he was not fed on time. Birju was supposed to be given half a can of Isocal formula every three hours. Often the aide forgot or got too busy to do so, then came and gave him a full can. The full can was too much food. Birju's face turned purple when this happened. We cranked up the top of his bed in case he vomited. Often he did. He'd open his mouth as if to burp. The Isocal, white and smelling of medicine and without the vinegar of gastric juices, would gush out along with whatever medications he had been given, including his beclamide, which kept him from having convulsions.

This was frightening because convulsions could cause more brain damage. My mother screamed at an aide once. The aide had given Birju a whole can and was still standing by the side of the bed as Birju vomited. "What does this mean?" she screamed. "What about the beclamide? Do we have to give him the beclamide again?" My mother's fists were clenched, and she was leaning forward. "Do you know? Do you think we'll be able to get a doctor to tell us? How long will it take to find out?"

Often I imagined being a gangster. I imagined looking like Amitabh Bachchan and beating the nurse's aides and having them spend all night sitting trembling in Birju's room.

After the settlement, we began visiting other nursing homes to see if we could move Birju to one of them. The first home we went to was in Connecticut. It cost $160,000 a year, but we went so we could see what such a home was like. We drove there on a January afternoon, crossing bridges and driving on wide, sunny highways.

The nursing home was up a long private road lined with trees. The road led to a vast lawn. A large yellow house surrounded by a porch looked out over the lawn.

The house was bigger inside than it appeared from the outside. There were hallways that seemed to run the length of a football field.

We were shown around by a woman in her fifties. She had blond hair and wore a wool suit buttoned with large buttons to the neck. As we walked down the hall on either side of her, the woman explained the therapy programs the home used. Every patient had physical therapy every day from a therapist, not an aide. Every patient also received stimulation therapy including speech therapy.

My mother, sounding nervous, asked, "Have you ever had a patient like Birju start talking?"

The woman stopped. She looked at my mother. "I am sorry. I wish I had." She paused again. "The oral therapy is so that the patient's ability to swallow doesn't diminish."

As we continued down the hall, the woman pointed to a nurses' station, a counter in the hallway. "Each station has a computer."

My father had his hands behind his back, as if we were in an expensive store and he didn't want anyone to think he might steal something. In the car, he had said to my mother that there was no point in going to a place we could not afford.

My father asked the woman, "Do you use those pads that let the nurses know if the patient has soiled himself?"

"Yes."

My mother told the woman about how Birju didn't get his food on time and then he vomited his medicines. "That shouldn't happen," the woman said. "That is unacceptable." Perhaps because my mother looked distressed, the woman said, "Beclamide is quickly absorbed. He probably doesn't lose too much."

Everything about the home was wonderful. Around every corner was a nurses' station with women in white uniforms. Everywhere we went, there was the smell of potpourri instead of the sour odor of recently cleaned shit. The hallway walls had black streaks at the height of wheelchair wheels and chipped paint at the height of gurneys, but these were minor things.

I thought about the three hundred thousand that the lawyers had taken. I thought that if Birju had not had his accident, he would have become a surgeon, and we would have been able to afford the home.

At some point I fell behind my parents. I started walking with my eyes closed. I swung my head from side to side and twirled in circles as I walked.

"Go outside," my mother scolded. "Don't leave the porch."

The porch was covered in black rubber matting. I left it and went onto the lawn. I found a branch and began dragging it around the house. The house flashed its windows at me and I felt as if it knew we could not afford to bring Birju there and yet were wasting people's time.

We went to other homes. Going to a home was like being on holiday. We were not at the nursing home with Birju but we were also doing our duty, and so there wasn't the guilt that came from being away from him.

Once, we went to a home in Boston. The home was a series of row houses along a wide road. Inside one, a young man with a blond mustache took us on a tour. On a stairway landing that had blue Wet Paint signs on the walls, we met a nurse, a very fat woman with a port-wine stain on her cheek. The young man introduced her. The nurse said, "I wouldn't put anybody from my family here. They say they give stimulation therapy every day. All they do is put patients in a room together and turn on the TV. Animal shelters do the same." While the nurse was speaking, the young man smiled and stared blankly at the wall behind my parents and the woman.

The nicest trip we ever took was to New Hope, Pennsylvania. New Hope was a tourist town, with little houses that spread up one side of a river valley. The nursing home was like most nursing homes: it had a sunny cafeteria where old people damaged from strokes sat in wheelchairs spitting food, and hallways that had closed doors with signs that the person within had pneumonia.

Once we had seen the home, we went for a walk around the town. There were ice cream shops and shops selling tee shirts. I saw something called an invisible dog leash. The waves against the river embankment sounded like window blinds lifting and falling in the wind, and the water, disturbing the reflections of the clouds, resembled waves slipping over ice floes.

MY PARENTS BEGAN to speak of buying a house where they could take care of Birju themselves.

"Even if we found a good nursing home, I would have to go there every day," my mother said.

Mr. Narayan sat by Birju's bed. It was a weekend afternoon. "Living with him sounds very hard," he said meekly.

"It isn't fair for Birju's mother to have to come every day," my father said. He was standing and drinking tea. "How long can she do this? She has to have a life, too."

Mr. Narayan didn't answer. He was quiet for a moment, and he looked like he was concentrating earnestly, trying to comprehend something that was beyond him. When he spoke, he sounded hesitant. "Still, it sounds very hard."

"If we don't come every day," my mother said, "he will get bed sores, he will get infections, he'll die. We have no choice. Either we do everything, or we do nothing."

A few days later, after prayers at temple, Mr. Narayan introduced us to a real estate agent. Mr. Gupta was tall, muscular, handsome. He had a ring on every finger, and to me, because I assumed they were worn for luck, he looked superstitious, as business people tend to be. Mr. Narayan said that Mr. Gupta would help us and not charge a commission. Mr. Gupta said, "It would be a blessing for me if I can be of help."

At this generosity, my mother began telling him how terrible our life was. "I get so scared every morning," she said. "When I walk into the nursing home, I think, *What am I going to discover today?*" My mother did not normally complain to strangers, but perhaps she assumed that somebody willing to do us such a favor must feel a great deal of sympathy and so she could be honest.

Mr. Gupta stood silently, politely before us.

"Thank you," my father said.

A few days later, we went with Mr. Gupta to look at houses. Mr. Gupta owned a blue Mercedes sedan. None of us had ever sat in a Mercedes before. This was exciting.

My father got into the front passenger seat, and my mother and I got in the back. It was a Saturday afternoon in spring.

As we drove, apropos of nothing, my father said, "Mr. Gupta, the tastiest food I've ever eaten was cooked over dung fire."

Mr. Gupta didn't say anything. He stared ahead as he drove slowly, his hands near the top of the steering wheel.

"I think there is something about dung that makes flavors sweet."

My father looked at Mr. Gupta as if he wanted a reaction. There was an eagerness to his face, and I could tell that he felt important because he was riding in a Mercedes and was going to spend thousands of dollars.

"I think so, too," Mr. Gupta finally said, switching on the turn signal. "I've told my children this. 'Dung!' they say. 'Eeew!'"

"I like simple things. Simple things are sufficient. A roti, some pickle, maybe a dry subji. That is enough."

"The best things are simple," Mr. Gupta agreed. "I don't like rich things with cheese. You have to stay up half the night digesting."

"Happiness can only be found inside oneself. It can't be found on the outside in expensive things. You hear that, Ajay?"

My mother stared out the window.

"Did you hear?"

"Yes, Daddy."

"I worry about India," my father said to Mr. Gupta.

"Why is that, Mr. Mishra?"

"Even the smallest things people don't do. Mahatma Gandhi advised, after you relieve yourself, just cover it with a little dirt so the flies don't spread disease. Does anybody do that? That's the kind of people India has."

"I hate to say it, but it's true." Mr. Gupta said this without emotion. To me he appeared to be agreeing because this was the polite thing to do.

My father kept talking. "It's not so much that we are better than whites, but that the people who come from India to America are the best Indians."

We visited several houses that day. It was strange to go into bathrooms and to think that a white man had stood in the tub, that the dirt and smell of meat that had covered the white man had been rinsed into the tub. It was strange to walk on carpets and to think that the bare feet of white people had walked over them. I kept expecting to find a *Playboy* magazine on a coffee table.

After that first Saturday, we began visiting houses for sale every weekend. One afternoon, we were in a house whose owner had already moved away. He had left behind his furniture. I stood in the kitchen. It had a sliding glass door. My parents were outside on the small back lawn. I could see them talking to Mr. Gupta but couldn't hear them. The kitchen was completely furnished. There was a table, a toaster oven, a coffeemaker, a wooden block with knives in it. Standing there I had the sudden realization that probably we would never go back to India, that probably we would live in America forever. The realization disturbed me. I saw that one day I would be nothing like who I was right then. I felt all alone.

I had not told anyone at school about Birju. I had been afraid that if I did, they would misunderstand in the same way that the women at the Ramayan Path had misunderstood, and then their confusion would remind me that what had happened to Birju did not matter for most of the world.

One morning, while the teacher was taking attendance, I leaned over my desk toward Jeff, the boy who sat in front of me. "Hey," I hissed. "I have a brother. When I said I didn't have a brother, I was lying." Jeff turned around. He had a pale oval face, sandy hair, and a nose that came to a point. "My brother's name is Birju. Birju. My brother is fifteen, almost sixteen. He had an accident in a swimming pool. He jumped into a pool and bumped his head on the bottom and was underwater for three minutes. He became brain damaged. He's in a nursing home near Menlo Park Mall. This happened nearly two years ago. It happened in August. Not last August, the August before." I said all of this in a rush, feeling scared, feeling almost like I was watching myself from the outside. "I'm sorry I lied to you."

For a moment Jeff looked at me silently. Then he nodded. "That's all right," he said. "Just don't do it again." He turned away to face the front of the class.

Mr. Esposito called Jeff's name. Jeff raised his arm and said, "Here." Mr. Esposito then called my name and I too raised my arm.

As attendance continued, I looked at the back of Jeff's head. Beneath his light brown hair was very white skin. My heart was racing. I wanted Jeff to turn around and express pity. Attendance ended. Mr. Esposito asked us to take out our social studies textbook. The children around me began doing so. I leaned over my desk once more. "My brother was very smart," I said. "He had gotten into the Bronx High School of Science. The Bronx High School of Science is one of the best schools in the country."

Jeff nodded. The back of his head went up and down.

Above the blackboard was a banner with capital and lower-case letters side-by-side: AaBbCc. Big brother, little brother.

I sat back in my chair. I had decided to tell Jeff because I was so unhappy, because everything was terrible, and because I had thought that if I told him about Birju, he would pity me and become my friend. Now I had the feeling that I had wasted something.

After school, I stood on the sidewalk and waited for my mother. She picked me up in our station wagon. At the nursing home, the door to Birju's room was open with the blinds raised and the lights on. We left Birju's room this way so that Birju would be easier to see from the corridor, in case something went wrong.

My mother entered Birju's room. She yelled, "Hello, lazy! Hello, smelly!"

Birju jerked in place. The springs of the bed squeaked.

"Fatso!" I shouted as I walked in behind her, and Birju jerked once more.

"Look at what your brother calls you," my mother said. She pulled Birju up by the shoulders and slid a second pillow under his head.

"Fatty! Fatty!" I cried.

"Tell him, 'I'm no fatty.'"

Birju was chewing his mustache. His face was swollen and almost square from medication. "Fatty, fatty," I said. I smiled and wagged my head. Pretending to be younger than I was, too young to notice Birju's gruesomeness, always seemed the proper way to behave.

My mother spread a newspaper over Birju's chest. Sitting sidesaddle on the bed, she began feeding him pureed bananas using a long spoon that was coated in rubber. "Yum, yum," she said as she pressed the spoon to Birju's mouth. Birju smacked his lips, took the mush into his mouth, and then puffed it onto the newspaper.

I saw this and thought, *Even a baby swallows what it likes.* Immediately, cool guilt slid over me like a cloud's shadow.

· · ·

I WAS AT THE school playground the next morning, waiting for the starting bell, when Jeff came up to me. He had a book bag dangling from one shoulder and both hands in his back pockets. He said, "Have you ever asked your brother to blink once for yes and twice for no?"

One of the reasons I had not told anyone was because I was afraid of questions like this. "I have. It doesn't work." Even as I had tried this in the hospital, with nobody else around, I had known that it would have no effect.

"Have you ever shouted 'Fire!' and run away and then seen if he would get up?"

"No," I murmured.

Jeff stared. "That might work."

"I'll try." I was quiet for a little while. Jeff remained standing before me. I said, "My brother was a genius. He took French for two weeks and after that he could speak it perfectly."

Jeff nodded. He looked serious, like he was being given a secret mission.

The school doors opened. Jeff and I went inside together.

At lunch I sat down across from him and his best friend, Michael Bu, a Chinese boy with a round face and sharp little teeth like a fish. "Can your brother not talk at all," Michael asked, "or does he sound retarded?"

My face became hot. I had considered asking Jeff not to tell anyone about Birju, but it had seemed too much to ask. "Not at all."

"What does he look like?" Michael asked.

I put a tater tot in my mouth and pointed a finger at my lips.

"What's wrong with your brother?" Mario asked. Mario was sitting next to Michael. Mario was very tall and wide. He had fuzz on his upper lip. Once, when the class sang, "You Are My Sunshine," he had cried. The children sometimes mocked him by singing the song.

"He had an accident in a swimming pool and became brain damaged."

"Does he open his eyes?" Mario asked.

"Yes."

Jeff said, "I saw a television show where a woman sees a murder and goes unconscious."

I pursed my lips to appear serious. "That happens."

"How does he eat?" Jeff asked.

I began to feel attacked.

"There is a tube in his stomach." I told them about the Isocal formula and the gastrointestinal tube. I said, "My brother was a great basketball player. He played two games and immediately got so good that he began beating people. When he played, people came to watch." By lying, I felt that I had placed a finger on a balance that was tilting too far to one side.

Within a few days, everybody in class had heard about Birju. Still, boys and girls came up to me during recess and asked eagerly whether I had a brother, as if the secret could be revealed once more.

Whenever I told someone about Birju, I felt compelled to lie about his wonderfulness. Because we had received so little money in the settlement, which meant that Birju was an ordinary boy, lying seemed the only way to explain that what had happened to him was awful, was the worst thing in the world. Birju, I said, had rescued a woman trapped in a burning car. Birju had had a great talent for music and a photographic memory.

Sometimes I didn't tell these lies, but only imagined them. I concocted an ideal brother. I took the fact that Birju had told our parents that I was being bullied and turned this into him being a karate expert who had protected me by beating up various boys. These fantasies felt real. They excited me. They made me love Birju and when I was in his room kiss his hands and cheeks. They also cultivated rage at the loss, the way my father's claims of racism cultivated it for him.

A part of me was anxious about the lies I told. I was afraid of being caught or doubted. Also, making up these stories seemed to serve as evidence that Birju had not been good enough for what happened to him to count as terrible. Each morning I woke on the sofa thinking of the lies I had told. Often I didn't want to go to school.

At some point, I became aware that Jeff no longer believed my lies. Yet when I came up to him on the playground before school, loyalty demanded that I keep lying. "Birju solved a math problem that professors hadn't been able to solve for years," or, "My brother was a very fast runner. Once, he threw a ball straight ahead of him, and he chased it and caught it

before it hit the ground." One morning, when I stood outside
school and told Jeff a lie, he stepped back and rolled his eyes.

IN MAY, WE put down our deposit on a house and told the
nursing home that we were taking Birju away. The evening
of that day, once we had finished dinner, my father put on his
shoes to leave.

"You don't need to go," my mother said, still sitting on the
floor. She said it quietly, looking up at him.

"Stop bothering me."

After he was gone, I put the dishes in the sink, threw the
newspaper in the trash can, and sat down on the sofa with
a stack of *Time* magazines I had borrowed from the school
library. I read *Time* as training, because it was boring and
because I needed to be able to do boring things now that we
would be caring for Birju. I read an article about the sound
quality of LP records compared to that of CDs. I read a book
review of a rich person's biography. Supposedly the rich man
was so cheap that he wouldn't order desserts at restaurants
because restaurants provided sweets for free at the ends of
dinners. I wondered what kinds of restaurants these were.

My mother came and sat down at the other end of the sofa
with her bag of sewing. Around ten, there was scratching at
the door, metal on metal. We had heard this once before.

That time my father had turned on the lights and stood by the door. He had shouted, "Who is it?" and kicked the door until the burglar went away.

Now, my mother stood by the door. "Who's there?" she demanded.

There was a chuckle in the hallway. It sounded like my father. My mother yanked the door open. He was crouched in the hallway, trying to fit his key into the keyhole.

He came into the apartment. He walked toward the sofa and half fell onto it.

"Get me some water," my father said. I went to the sink and poured him a glass.

My mother said, "Come lie down." She helped him up and led him to the mattress behind the sofa. I brought the glass and handed it to my mother.

A few days later, on Friday night at temple, many different people came and tried to touch my parents' feet. The news had spread that we were taking Birju out of the nursing home.

"Get up. Get up," my mother said to a woman bending down before her.

My father said, more roughly, "There is no reason for this."

At school, I told Jeff that I had seen a swami cause a rope to levitate, and then the swami had climbed the rope and vanished into the sky. I told Jeff that I had seen a swami who was thirsty knock on a wall, and the wall spout water.

One day at lunch I told Jeff and Michael Bu a fairy tale that my grandfather had told me and I claimed that it had happened to my uncle. I told them that one of my uncles in India could speak the language of birds. This uncle had overheard two crows discussing a murder. As I told the story, I leaned forward over the lunch table, feeling the usual panic in my face. "My uncle went to the police station to tell them. The policemen he talked to thought that the only person who could know what my uncle was saying was the murderer, and so they arrested him."

Michael asked, "Do Indian crows speak the same language as American crows?"

The question baffled me. I sat there silently for a moment. Then, not knowing how to reply, I answered, "Chow wow, eat dog lo mein."

JEFF AND MICHAEL began to show their dislike openly. It was now June and hot. In the mornings, when I would try to join them in some ordinary conversation, such as last night's episode of The A-Team, they would turn their backs on me and keep talking. Once, I came up to them on the playground, and they just walked away. When I walked after them, they went faster and began laughing.

One lunch period, I sat down across from Jeff and Michael in the cafeteria and said, "We're starting to move the furniture that we've bought. We'll move to our house right after school ends, and then Birju will be brought a few days later."

Jeff and Michael went on with their conversation.

"I'm going to take French next year," Michael said, keeping his eyes directly on Jeff.

"I'm going to take French, too," I said. "My brother studied French." I remembered Birju calling me monsieur and how funny it had sounded.

"Spanish is more useful," Jeff said, looking at Michael.

"France is a more important country than Spain," I answered.

"Do you hear something? I don't hear anything," Michael said.

"The Spanish teacher seems nicer," said Jeff.

I said, "On Saturday mornings, nurse's aides come to Birju's room and shave his crotch. They do this because of Birju's urinary catheter. The catheter looks like a condom. To keep it from slipping off, they have to tape it. They don't want the tape to get caught in the hair." Jeff and Michael stared at me. They appeared shocked.

"When they do that," Michael said, "does your brother's dick get hard?"

Speaking calmly, like I was talking about some ordinary thing, I said, "Birju's G-tube needs to be changed every six weeks. It needs to be changed or he gets infections. The G-tube is actually two tubes next to each other. The G-tube goes in here." I pressed two fingers to the right side of my stomach. "One tube is thin and longer than the other and has a balloon at the end. Once both tubes are in Birju's stomach, the doctor fills the balloon with water. This keeps the tubes from sliding out. The thick tube is what the food goes through. To change Birju's tube, the doctor takes the water out of the balloon and slides out the tubes." Jeff and Michael were staring at me, and my voice got higher and higher as I told this awful truth. "When the doctor puts in the new tube, the tube sometimes misses the hole in the stomach. It scratches the outside of the stomach." I lifted up the two fingers I had been holding against my side. I bent them into a hook and scratched the air. "Sometimes the outside of the stomach starts bleeding."

Later, during science class, with the lights off because Mrs. Salt was showing a video, I leaned all the way over my desk till my lips were right next to Jeff's ear. I whispered, "Birju had some X-rays recently, and we discovered that he had broken three ribs a while ago. Maybe some aide dropped him off the bed one night and didn't tell anyone. For months we moved him and exercised him when he had broken ribs." Speaking the truth made me feel powerful.

The next morning, I went up to Michael on the playground. He was talking to a boy, and without saying hello, I said, "The patients at the nursing home are always getting sick, and the antibiotics give them diarrhea." Michael stared at me, confused. "Sometimes this happens at night, and the nurse's aide doesn't clean the person. There are acids in the shit, and if the person isn't cleaned till morning, the acids cut the skin right here." I was wearing shorts, and I used both hands to rub the insides of my thighs.

"You're a freak," Michael said.

"It's the truth," I answered. To say the horrible truth and to know that I had seen unbearable things, made me feel that I was strong and Michael was weak.

Fifteen minutes later, inside my classroom, all of us stood by our desks and said the Pledge of Allegiance. I stood with my hand over my heart, and Jeff did the same thing two feet in front of me.

Once the pledge was done, before we took our seats, I told Jeff about the naked girl. "She's down the hall from my brother. She's eighteen or nineteen. Her boyfriend strangled her, and when he thought she was dead, he put her in a closet. She didn't die. She became brain damaged." Jeff turned around and glared. "Nobody comes to see her, so she's almost always naked. They only dress you at the nursing home if they think you'll have visitors. Otherwise, it's too much work because the people who live there are always soiling themselves. Sometimes the door to her room is open. Her pussy has black hair. The hair looks like ants."

I finished speaking. Jeff didn't say anything. I had been nervous and I became even more so. I put a hand on my desk and tried leaning casually against it. Jeff punched me in the middle of my chest. I felt as if a wave had gone over me. I stumbled backward and fell.

Mr. Esposito skipped lightly across the room. He grabbed Jeff's wrist. Jeff's hand was still clenched. Mr. Esposito shook Jeff's wrist till the fist opened.

I pushed myself onto my knees and stood. "I fell," I said.

· · ·

THAT SATURDAY MY father and I went to Jeff's house, a blue ranch-style home with vinyl siding and cement steps that rose up to a cement platform and a screen door. Behind this was a blue wooden door.

The door opened, and there stood a tall, slender woman in black jeans.

"I'm Rajinder Mishra," my father said. I had brought my father there because I felt that perhaps Jeff did not appreciate how terrible it was to have Birju the way he was, and if somebody else told him about Birju, he might then perhaps become sympathetic. I had told my father that Jeff did not believe that I had a brother in a nursing home and that it was important that he understand. "Ajay," my father said, glancing down, "is a friend of Jeff's."

I held up two Superman comic books. Returning these was the excuse for visiting. "They're Jeff's."

Jeff's mother led us into a kitchen with blue counters and cupboards. Several brown grocery bags sat on the counters near the refrigerator. Mrs. Miles shouted, "Jeff!" She then asked my father if he would like some coffee.

"Could I have water?" My father's lips were white and chapped from the dehydration of his drinking.

Jeff's mother poured him a glass, and my father drank it quickly.

Mrs. Miles opened the refrigerator and began emptying the grocery bags into it. My father and I stood silently side by side.

After a moment, my father said, "Your son has been very kind to Ajay." Mrs. Miles looked over her shoulder and smiled.

My father put his hand on the back of my neck. I sensed that he was about to talk about Birju, and I regretted having brought him.

"My other son, Ajay's older brother, had an accident in a swimming pool and was severely brain damaged two years ago. Two years this August."

"I'm sorry," Mrs. Miles said. She closed the refrigerator door and turned toward us. She had blue eyes and a strong, masculine jaw. She looked serious and handsome.

"We had only been in America two years when it happened. Ajay is sensitive. Your son has been a good friend."

"Jeff's a sweetheart," Mrs. Miles said.

"Ajay's sensitive, and it's difficult for him to make friends."

Mrs. Miles opened her mouth to say something. Jeff came into the kitchen. He was wearing gray sweatpants and a white undershirt. There was a diagonal crease on one cheek as if he had been lying on it. Jeff saw us, paused midstep, rolled his eyes, and kept moving forward.

I tugged my father's hand and said, "We have to go."

"We brought your comics," my father said, smiling and pointing to where they lay on the counter. "I was just telling your mother about Ajay's older brother. Ajay's older brother had an accident in a swimming pool and is brain damaged."

Jeff went to the grocery bags and, standing on his toes, peered into one.

I tugged at my father again.

We left the house.

Outside it was hot and humid. We walked back toward our apartment through the town's nice neighborhood. The houses that lined the road were large and set back, some behind tall oaks.

"He's stupid not to believe you."

I didn't say anything. I peered at the trees and the houses beyond them. I wanted my father to not talk.

"People are stupid, crazy," he said. "A woman came up to me at temple and said, 'I wouldn't mind my son being sick if I got a lot of money like you.'" He raised his voice. "Vineeta buaji said we were being emotional. That's why we were taking Birju out of the nursing home. I said, 'If I'm not emotional about my own son, who am I going to be emotional about?'"

We came to a red traffic light and stopped. "You have to ignore people like that Jeff boy. Expecting sympathy from somebody like that is like expecting sympathy from dirt."

The day Birju was supposed to be brought to our house, Mr. Narayan rang our doorbell at around eight in the morning. He stood in the doorway smiling, his face eager. "I thought you might have work for me," he said.

More people came. The morning was very bright. Cars filled our driveway and then others parked on the street along our lawn. As the doorbell rang and rang again, the excitement of having visitors gave the day some of the festiveness of Diwali in India when people, dressed formally, visit from morning till evening.

The ambulance arrived around eleven. The cars in the driveway backed out. When the ambulance was parked, two orderlies, a large black man and a smaller white one, tugged Birju out of the ambulance on a stretcher and brought him up the cement path that curved from the bottom of the driveway to the front door.

Birju's room was the former dining room. It had yellow walls, a hardwood floor, and a chandelier with plastic candles hanging from the center of the ceiling. A hospital bed stood along a wall with a narrow window beside where Birju's head would be. The orderlies rolled Birju into the room. They hefted him onto the bed. The people visiting stood against the walls. When he was on the bed, Birju raised his head and moaned, and turned his head this way and that, like he was trying to look through his darkness. My mother leaned over my brother and whispered, "You're home." She stroked his face, kissed his forehead. "Your Mommy is here." I stood and watched. My chest hurt. I wondered, *What now?*

The orderlies left. Mr. Narayan joined my parents at the bedside. They stared at Birju. Birju's chin and cheeks were covered in saliva. The window was open, and its lace curtain drifted up trembling in the air. Mr. Narayan, looking moved, turned to my father. "Tell us what you want," he said, "and we'll obey."

My father stared at my brother. His face appeared swollen. He seemed stunned. I worried that he would complain. I wanted us to be dignified.

Later, in the afternoon, in the kitchen, the women sat at the table and cut vegetables and sang prayers. The men did heavier work. They installed two air conditioners and lifted the washer in the laundry room and placed it on bricks. From outside came the roar of a lawn mower as one of the men cut the grass. All this activity made our house feel like a tem-

ple being gotten ready for a festival, when the people of the
neighborhood gather and mop the floor and string flowers
into garlands. Having so many visitors gave me the sense that
my family was important.

People kept arriving until nine or ten that night.

THE NEXT DAY began with a bath for Birju. I came downstairs around six. Birju was lying naked on his hospital bed.
My father was rubbing him down with coconut oil.

We had given Birju sponge baths before but never a bath in
a tub. "Hello, fatty," I called out. I smiled. I walked boldly. I
was nervous. The room was bright, and my mother was there,
too, near the bed, spreading a towel over the back and seat of
the wheelchair.

My mother looked over her shoulder at me. "Birju, say, 'I'm
your older brother. Speak with respect.'" She was smiling. She
moved quickly, and her glass bracelets jingled as she smoothed
the towel. Because I was pretending to be cheerful, I assumed
she was acting, too.

I stood at the foot of the bed. Birju's pubic hair was shaved
to stubble. His stomach was a dome, and his G-tube, bound
in a figure eight, resembled a ribbon on the side of a girl's
head. "Brother," I said, "I have never met anyone as lazy as
you. Making people bathe you."

My mother, finishing with the towel, straightened herself. "Tell him, 'I'm not lazy. I'm a king.'"

My father slipped his arms through Birju's underarms. He pulled him up until Birju was half sitting. My father grinned. He leaned down and said into Birju's ear. "Why are you so heavy? Are you getting up at night and eating? You are, aren't you? Admit it. I see crumbs on your chin."

I laughed. I grabbed Birju's legs below the knees. My mother rolled the wheelchair next to the bed, and my father and I counted to three. We swung him into it. My father began pulling the wheelchair backward through the room. He pulled it out a doorway and across a narrow hall, into the bathroom.

The bathroom had a tub with a small bathing chair inside. My father put one leg into the tub and kept one leg out. He put his arms through Birju's underarms. Again, we counted. "One, two, three." My father yanked and twisted, and I lifted. We hefted and slid Birju onto the chair.

My father held an arm across Birju's chest to keep him from toppling forward. I took a red mug and poured warm water over Birju's head. He began to relax. His legs, which had been sticking out toward the tap, eased down. I poured water over his shoulders and arms. My father rubbed Birju's neck with soap. He lathered his shoulders. Birju started urinating, a thick, strong-smelling, yellow stream. When Birju finished peeing, my father bent him forward. He shoved a bar of soap in the split between Birju's buttocks. Gray water and flecks of shit dropped into the tub.

I chattered. "I dreamt I was fighting twenty people. I hit one. He fell over. I hit another. He fell over. It was fun." I kept talking and talking. I was smiling, for I wished it to appear that I wasn't seeing what was occurring before me.

Around noon, my father and I went to the pharmacy. This intimidated me. I had seen my father scream at my mother about how much things would cost. I was scared of spending money. I felt that once money was spent, it would be gone forever and couldn't be replaced.

The pharmacy was on Main Street, a few shops from the train station. The store had a glass front. In the back was a high counter where one submitted one's prescriptions and where the store owner sat.

I stood with outstretched arms near the counter. My father put a case of Isocal formula in my arms. Then he placed another on top of this.

"How do you want to pay?" the store owner said.

"Put it on my tab," my father answered and to me, in Hindi, said, "Move."

I turned around and began hurrying.

"No," the store owner, a slender white-haired man with a goatee, called. I stopped and turned back around.

My father signed a receipt. He signed it with his left hand, the pen moving awkwardly and not making full contact with the paper. I believed he was signing with his left hand so that perhaps he could deny that it was his signature.

When we came back to the house, we had lunch. It was strange to eat on a plate at a table instead of, as at the nursing home, on a sheet of aluminum foil balanced on our pressed-together knees. All day that day, walking around the house barefoot, I noticed the feeling of the kitchen linoleum or the soft carpet of the living room and suddenly remembered that at the home I would be wearing shoes. Each time, the feeling of freedom was like the beginning of summer vacation, when one looks at a clock and is amazed, all over again, not to be in school.

I kept going to look at Birju, but I couldn't get used to seeing him in an ordinary room in an ordinary house. Every time, I was startled.

Birju was restless. He ground his teeth, and his eyes darted around.

At some point in the late afternoon, I decided to go outside and throw a ball. This seemed like something any ordinary boy might do.

Outside, it was bright and humid. I stood in the center of our front lawn and flung a fluorescent green tennis ball straight into the air. It went higher than our brown shingle roof, and came down more slowly than it rose. The sky was so pretty and blue that it was like something from a cartoon. I caught the ball and spun in place. I threw it again and bent my knees catching it. I threw it one more time and tried catching the ball behind my back. I missed. The ball went bounding away.

I threw the ball over and over, sometimes with my left hand. When I did this, the ball went up at a slant.

Throwing the ball, I didn't feel any better. I kept seeing Birju lying on his bed, his head tilted up, the white curtain on the window beside him rising and falling.

My tee shirt grew damp and stuck to my skin. Before long I wanted to go back inside, but to go inside felt like giving up. I stayed on the lawn and threw the ball.

THROUGH AN AGENCY we hired a nurse's aide to read to Birju and exercise him. This aide came at eight in the morning and left at four. Another came at night, from ten until six. Then, after a week or two, miracle workers who said they could wake Birju began arriving. We were sometimes able to save money by dispensing with the day aide.

Some of the miracle workers were the same ones who had visited us in the nursing home. The first was Mr. Mehta. By profession, he was a petroleum engineer, but Mr. Mehta was unemployed. He would come at nine in the morning. Each of his visits started with him flinging a saffron-colored sheet over Birju, who lay on his exercise bed, a tall wooden platform that spent most of the day beneath the room's chandelier.

After he straightened and smoothed the sheet, Mr.

Mehta would kneel down beside Birju and begin to pray. He would pray for fifteen minutes or so, hands pressed tightly together. Slender, balding, dark-skinned, he always wore gray dress pants and black socks. The saffron sheet was printed with oms and swastikas. When Mr. Mehta finished praying, he would stand and begin to make his way around the bed, pulling out an arm or a leg from beneath the sheet and rubbing it vigorously till the hair stood on end. Once the hair was standing, he would put the limb back under the sheet. When he reached Birju's head, he would rub his hands together and clap them to Birju's ears. He'd cry, "Aum namah Shivaya."

I thought Mr. Mehta was strange, but I had heard my mother listen patiently to many strange things.

At the end of Mr. Mehta's first day, my mother asked him, "Do you notice any difference?" She was standing in the vestibule that the front door opened onto. Mr. Mehta was sitting on the stairs putting on his shoes.

"Everything takes time," he said. He smiled as if he were a teacher and my mother a nervous student who needed to be calmed and told to be patient.

"But any difference?"

"Don't worry, ji. We will return your son to you."

As she stood looking at him, my mother's face appeared small and meek. It occurred to me that my mother was taking Mr. Mehta seriously. This surprised me. Until that moment, I had thought that we were allowing him into the house because if a potential cure was free and caused no harm, then why not attempt it?

Once Mr. Mehta was gone, my mother perched on the exercise bed and began feeding Birju pureed bananas with a long spoon. Newspapers were spread over his chest. My mother maneuvered the spoon between Birju's teeth and said, "Eat, baby, eat. Eat, or Ajay will take your food."

Looking at her, I remembered that earlier in the day, when Mr. Mehta arrived, my mother had been very excited. She had told him, "If you return Birju to how he was, I will sit at your feet the rest of my life." I had taken this for politeness, since if someone comes to perform a cure and doesn't ask for money, the least one can do is pretend to believe.

I watched my mother feed Birju. He drooled clots of gray mush. Periodically she wiped his chin with a hand towel. After several minutes, I said, "Mommy, do you think Birju could get better?"

"God can do anything," she said, keeping her eyes on Birju.

My father came home at six. He stood in Birju's room drinking tea, sweating lightly. I went and stood beside him. I pressed my head against his waist.

My thoughts were jumbled. Hearing my mother say that Birju could get better had scared me. It had made me feel all alone.

My father smelled a little of hard alcohol being sweated out, something like nail polish remover evaporating. "Full of love are you?" he asked. He patted my head.

A little later, my father and I swung Birju into his wheel-

chair and rolled him backward into the kitchen, to the head
of the kitchen table. My father began to feed Birju a puree of
the roti and lentils that we would be eating a little later. Birju
took some of the food into his mouth and spat the rest onto
his chest. I had seen this many times before, but on the evening of Mr. Mehta's first visit, I turned my head away.

Most nights, my mother and I played cards. My father would
be upstairs in his room and my mother and I sat on either side
of Birju's bed and dealt for three, placing the discards on Birju's chest and stomach. The television in the corner would play
Jeopardy. As we handled the cards, we cheated. We had Birju
throw away his best cards. Sometimes we just stole them. That
night especially, I felt the need to act very brave. I spoke loudly.
I teased Birju. "Pay attention! Playing with you is no fun." We
played until about ten, when the night aide came.

THE NEXT DAY and the day after and the day after that,
Mr. Mehta worked diligently, moving briskly around the bed,
taking out a leg, rubbing it, tucking it under the sheet, moving
to the next leg, then up to an arm. Now and then my mother
would send me to Birju's room with a glass of Coke, which
Mr. Mehta drank in gulps.

All morning my mother would stay in the kitchen cooking
elaborate lunches for him. The steam cooker would huff, and
the pot of oil in which she fried puris would send up waves of

heat. The sight of my mother in the kitchen caused my chest to hurt. Her belief that Birju could get better made me feel that she didn't love us, that she valued believing something ridiculous over taking care of us, that she was willing to let us be hurt so she could have her hope.

One night, my father began shouting at my mother. This was in the kitchen. Birju was in the wheelchair. My father was drunk. His face was lax and his lips wet. "You couldn't try these cures at the nursing home and so you couldn't accept that Birju is dead."

"What are you talking about?" my mother demanded. She was standing at the stove. "You are drunk."

"Why am I drunk? Tell me—why am I drunk?"

My mother didn't respond.

"I am so unhappy, and you have no pity for me."

My mother became irritated. "If I lost a diamond earring," she hissed, "would I not look everywhere?"

As the days passed, I tried to spend more time with my father. In the evening, when he came home and sat on the radiator in the laundry room taking off his shoes, I boiled his tea. When he went to Birju's room, I followed with the tea and a plate of biscuits.

My father looked indifferent as he took these from me. I felt that his indifference was my fault, that I should have appreciated him more in the past.

At six thirty, we swung Birju into his wheelchair so that he could get his oral feeding. At eight, my father went upstairs to his and my mother's room to drink. Though we didn't talk much, it seemed to me that by making tea and being near him, I was sharing in his thoughts. I wanted us to be close, and so I began believing that we were.

When my father stood quietly in Birju's room, drinking his tea, I imagined that he was thinking about what he could do to make our life better. When he went upstairs to drink, I saw him choosing to be happy. It was, in my eyes, a mark of sophistication to find a way to be happy in a difficult situation.

In July I turned twelve.

Within a week of Mr. Mehta's first visit, the phone in the kitchen rang regularly with people who wanted to come and watch him at work. Some of the people who visited we knew. Others were strangers. They stood in Birju's room and watched the cure like tourists visiting a temple to see an exorcism.

"This is true fire sacrifice," a man said to my mother in Birju's room.

My mother said, "What choice do I have?" She looked embarrassed. She knew that the visitors saw her as slightly crazy but they found what she was doing noble and very Indian, and so this made them feel good about being Indian themselves, about going to temple, about doing things such as scolding their children when they got bad grades.

I brought the visitors cups of tea as they watched Birju. I was full of anger and shame as I did this. A few of them pressed dollar bills into my hands.

. . .

A<small>T SOME POINT</small> during his third week, Mr. Mehta's pace began to flag. When I brought him a glass of Coke, he sat down and sipped it slowly as if he were drinking something hot.

One afternoon, I was coming down the stairs when Mr. Mehta called out to me. He was standing by the exercise bed, holding one of Birju's arms in the air. "Do you ever get headaches?" he asked.

I knew Mr. Mehta wanted me to say yes. Speaking the truth automatically, though, I said, "No."

"Never?"

I was quiet for a moment. "Sometimes," I said hesitantly.

Mr. Mehta smiled. "Look at grass. If you spend ten minutes each day looking at something green, you'll never get headaches."

After this, whenever I came into Birju's room, Mr. Mehta would try to strike up a conversation. "Sit for a minute," he'd say. "Let me finish this."

I'd sit on a low table next to the hospital bed. Once Mr. Mehta had completed his circuit, he would sit on the hospital bed and talk. One time, he told me that on his first weekend in America, he had gone to a museum of oil production in Titusville, Pennsylvania. He had wanted to see this museum ever since he heard about it in college. "Did you know people used to drink oil because they thought it was good for them? Maybe it's true. In small doses."

Mr. Mehta had traveled the world. He had been to Rome.

"If we had broken buildings like that in Delhi, no whitey would say, 'Isn't this wonderful?'" Mr. Mehta had also been to Paris. "Every building there looks like Parliament House. It is the most beautiful city in the world. There is dog shit everywhere, though. What is the point of a city being so beautiful if you have to always be looking down?"

One morning, Mr. Mehta's small brown hatchback did not pull up in front of our lawn. At ten o'clock, my mother phoned his house. She sat at the kitchen table, the cordless phone to her ear and the phone's antenna outstretched. From where I stood, I could hear the high complaining voice of Mrs. Mehta. She said Mr. Mehta was sick, and something in her tone suggested that we were stupid to call and inquire. The next day, my mother phoned again. The third day, as I watched my mother punch in the numbers, I felt helplessness that my mother wouldn't stop calling.

Mrs. Mehta's voice came sharp over the phone. "Yes, he is still sick," she said and hung up.

My mother turned toward me. Her face was tight. "Indians are that way. They are cowards. Instead of admitting they made a mistake, they would rather lie and try to blame you."

THE STRANGENESS OF the miracle workers made the days dreamlike. The next miracle worker was a white-skinned man with green eyes and a square flabby face. This man had been born in Kashmir and lived in Philadelphia. He told us that the drive to our house took two hours. As soon as he said this, I knew he wouldn't come for long.

On his first day, the man complained about the heat. My mother and I placed three table fans on the floor of Birju's room, their heads tilted up, turning side to side.

Regularly the man went outside to smoke on our front steps. As he smoked, he looked so angry that it was as if he had just been insulted. "My God," my mother said, "I feel frightened asking him to stand away from the house."

On his third day, the man arrived and, within an hour, said he was going out to smoke. Instead he walked down the steps, crossed the lawn to his car, got in, and drove away.

That night, during Birju's oral feeding, my mother told my father that she had no choice, that she had to try everything to wake Birju. "What kind of mother would I be if I don't try?"

My father didn't answer. He looked down at Birju's food smeared face.

"What kind of mother would I be?"

Again my father didn't respond.

"I am a mother," she said. It was as if she wanted a fight and so wouldn't stop talking.

"If there were a cure, Shuba," my father said finally, still keeping his eyes on my brother, "wouldn't it be in all the newspapers?"

After this man there was a woman who tried bathing Birju with turmeric powder. Birju began to look orange.

Then there was an elderly man who walked with a stoop. On his first day, he gave me eleven dollars. I felt embarrassed because I wanted the money but was afraid that by taking it I would give up my right to hate him.

This man's cure involved sitting by my brother and reading facts about him from a yellow legal pad. He would sit behind Birju's head and rest his hands on Birju's temples. This was to allow healing powers to flow from his body into my brother's. "My name is Birju Mishra. I was born on October 7, 1968. My favorite hobby is making model airplanes. My ambition is to be a surgeon. My best friend is Himanshu. I got into the Bronx High School of Science."

Eventually, the man grew bored with trying to wake Birju. At some point, he suggested that he teach me exercises for my back.

"My back is fine," I said.

My mother said, "When you're older, it won't be. Learn now."

The man had me lie on Birju's floor and raise my feet into the air and try touching my toes.

August fifth was the second anniversary of Birju's accident. That morning, when I woke up, I lay on my side. I couldn't believe that everything had changed because of three minutes.

One evening, not long after the anniversary, my father was

in Birju's room drinking tea. I came and stood next to him. I was very unhappy. My father must have sensed this. He patted my head quickly, and in his quickness I knew that there was both an acknowledgment of me and also a desire that I move away and not say anything. After a moment I said, "Daddy, I am so sad."

"You're sad?" my father said angrily. "I want to hang myself every day."

Birju was lying on his exercise bed. It was the first day of seventh grade and I had just come home. I saw my brother and began screaming. "Hello, fatty! Hello, smelly! Who have you been bothering today?" I was standing in the doorway that my father and I rolled Birju through each morning. I was grinning. "Do you think of anybody but yourself?" I shouted. "In my life I have never met anyone so selfish." It was a gray day. The chandelier was lit. Birju was wearing thin cotton pajamas. He was puffing spit, his eyes rolled back as if he were trying to remember something. "Smelly! Smelly!" I shouted. I didn't know why I was screaming. I felt possessed.

I walked up to the exercise bed. I took the washcloth that lay on Birju's chest and wiped his mouth and chin. The cloth caught on his stubble, and I had the feeling that I was hurting him. "All day you do nothing," I scolded. "All day you lie here and fart." A fear like cold seeped into me. "I have to go to school. I have to study and take tests." The more I talked, the more scared I got. It was as if my own voice was pumping fear into me.

Sitting in a folding chair with my elbows on the bed, I heard my voice growing shrill. "Birju brother, you are lucky not to go to school. In seventh grade, we walk from class to class. It isn't like elementary school where you stay in one room and teachers come to you." As I said this, I became aware that while for me, time passing meant new schools and new teachers, for Birju, it meant wearing thin cotton pajamas and then flannel ones. I became so afraid I hopped up.

I climbed into the exercise bed. I lay down next to Birju. I slipped an arm under his shoulders. Birju's breath smelled of vomit. He smacked his lips. He still looked lost in thought. Till that day, perhaps because Birju had been mostly in the hospital and nursing home and these had seemed temporary, some part of me had seen the difference between our lives as also temporary. Now, going to school and coming back home and seeing him, no part of me could deny how much luckier I was than my brother.

"Brother-life," I said, using the phrase because it was melodramatic and because by saying something melodramatic, I could make myself sound ridiculous, like a child, and so not to be blamed for my good luck of being OK, "my English teacher wanted us to write a paragraph on what we did during the summer. I didn't have a pencil. What kind of fool am I?" As I spoke, I had the feeling that I was being watched. I had the sense that some man was looking at me and that this man knew I was not very good and yet I had received so much of my family's luck. I began speaking in an even more childish voice. "I have homework. It's the first day of school, and I have homework. I wish I were back in first grade." As I spoke, I remembered Arlington. I remembered lying on my mattress and talking to God. The fact that nothing had changed, that Birju was still the way he was, that we still needed him to be OK to be OK ourselves, made me feel like I was being gripped and slowly crushed. "Wouldn't it be wonderful to get good marks without having to work? Brother-life, tomorrow you go to school and I'll stay home. I took a lunch box to school. In seventh grade, you don't take lunch boxes. Boys made fun of me."

Talking, talking, talking, I slowly began to get calmer.

THE NEXT MORNING, as I walked down the street to the corner where the school bus stopped, I pictured Birju the way I had left him, in his quiet, dim room, snoring on his back, his mouth open. I saw my mother, too. She was in the laundry room, stuffing the washing machine with the sheets and pillowcases from last night. Not only was I luckier than my brother, but I was also more fortunate than my mother. I wanted to shriek. While a part of me was glad I wasn't like my brother, no part of me wished to be more fortunate than my mother. To be luckier than her was to be different from her, it was to be apart from her, it was to have a life that would take me away from her.

At school, the guilt and sadness were like wearing clothes still damp from the wash. Whenever I moved, I felt as though I were touching something icy. In history class, I sat in the first desk of the fourth row. I learned that Andrew Jackson was called "Old Hickory." My knowing this meant that I had gained something, that I was being made rich while my mother and brother remained poor.

In school, there were twenty Indians among the five hundred or so students. Three or four of them spoke without accents and bought lunch or brought American-style sandwiches. The rest of us sat at the same long table in the cafeteria, the girls at one end and the boys at another. The white and black children abused us. Boys would walk past us and call, "Shit! I smell shit!" In my guilt and shame, I wanted to fight, to be nothing like myself. I shouted insults. "I fucked your mother in the ass. That's what you're smelling."

Once, a boy leaned over my shoulder and demanded to know what I was eating. I said I was eating snake. The boy believed me. He began shouting, "snake". A crowd gathered around me. I felt boys pressing against my back. Other boys stood on the benches of the long tables.

The vice principal, a short white-haired man, appeared. "What are you eating?" he demanded.

"Okra," I said.

"Come with me." He led me through the crowd, pushing the boys out of his way. He took me to detention hall, a room with white cinder block walls.

The recent immigrants at the lunch table found me annoying.

They saw me as a troublemaker for responding to the insults. To them, I was a show-off for not keeping quiet. This was true to an extent. Part of my motivation for fighting was that I did not want to be like the recent immigrants and so I was deliberately trying to be different. There were other ways that I was a show-off too. I often reminded the boys I sat with that I was in more advanced-level classes than they were. Sitting with these children, a part of me was surprised that not all Indians were smart.

Often in the evening, my mother and I would leave the house and go for walks. As we went down sidewalks, cars would drive past us and people would shout curses; haji, Gandhi, sand nigger. The first time this happened, I, for some reason, thought my mother would not understand that we were being cursed and so I told her that these were people I knew from school, that they were calling out to me in greeting. My mother nodded as if she believed me.

I began not wanting to go on these evening walks. When we did go, I carried stones in my pocket.

Weeks passed. The weather got colder. The days tipped backward into darkness. Some evenings our house and street appeared dark while the sky was light. In October the trees shed their leaves, and our house stood undefended on its lawn.

THE WORST THING about our new life with Birju was worrying about money. Now that I was going to school and the miracle workers had mostly stopped coming, we needed to hire a full-time nurse's aide during the day. We decided not to use the agency because the agency charged almost twelve dollars an hour and we thought we could get someone much cheaper. My father put advertisements in the local newspaper. The ads said that pay was based on experience.

A Filipino aide with long black hair came to be interviewed. She stood by the exercise bed. When she learned how much my mother intended to pay, she shouted, "Why not you tell me on the phone? Why you make me drive so long? You do this to a black, she burn your house down."

My heart jumped when she shouted at us. At the same time, I felt that it was OK to be shouted at as long as we did not spend the extra money.

The cold weather affected our plumbing. Some of our water came from a well. When the white washing machine shook and churned, the dim laundry room filled with a marshy smell.

In the kitchen one night, standing at the stove, my mother yelled, "I don't care how much it costs."

"You don't care because you don't pay the bills," my father yelled back.

"What are we going to do now?"

"You were the one to say buy the house. We've gotten cheated." The kitchen was very bright. My father said the new plumbing might cost five thousand dollars. The room hung reflected in the windows. My father started crying. I was stunned. What did it mean to spend five thousand dollars? The house had cost eighty-four thousand. I wondered if, in America, one could return a house the same way that one could return a belt to a store.

We also worried about the insurance. The insurance company said no to everything. They said no to the Isocal formula. They said no to the disposable blue pads that we put under Birju for when he soiled himself. They said no to the nurse's aides. On Saturday and Sunday afternoons, my father sat at the kitchen table and filled out insurance forms. On the table were rubber-banded stacks of letters, a stapler, his checkbook, and a yellow legal pad on which he wrote letters to the insurance company. My mother and I always kept very quiet while my father did this work.

SEVENTH GRADE WAS the first time we were divided into honors-level classes and accelerated levels and track one and track two. This was when I began to think that I was smart enough. I didn't think I was very smart—only that I had enough intelligence to get by. Even the idea of being smart upset me; it made me angry. I came home with my grades from the first quarter and saw Birju lying on his exercise bed and wondered what the point of all As was. Still, I was glad to be better than other boys.

My classes had mostly Jews, a few Chinese, and one or two Indians. The Indians were not Indian the way I was. They didn't have accents. They were invited to birthday parties by white children.

I preferred talking to the Jews over the Chinese or the Indians. The Jews were white, and so they seemed more valuable than these others. Also, with the Chinese and the Indians, I sensed they watched me with suspicion the same way I watched them, that since they knew immigrants, they understood that I was untrustworthy, that immigrants are desperate and willing to do almost anything.

ONE VERY COLD night in November, our front doorbell rang. We opened the door, and a jowly man was standing outside. Behind him was a tall boy in a long winter coat. We had met the man at temple, but we didn't know him well. We invited them in.

In the kitchen, the man stood wearing his ski jacket and in his stocking feet. The SAT was that weekend, and he asked my mother to bless his son. "Put your hand on his head, and it will be done." He spoke in a jolly tone, which was intended to make him seem simpleminded, someone with whom there was no point in arguing.

My mother looked surprised. She remained standing even though the polite thing would have been to sit so the man would know that we wanted him to stay. "Ji, what use is this?" she said. When people visited our house, they often asked my parents to bless their children. This was just out of politeness, though. I too often touched people's feet to show respect. What the man was doing was different. He was asking for a blessing so that something specific would occur and this felt closer to us being treated like we were holy.

"You may not believe in yourself, but the whole world believes in you." Again, there was a deliberate simplemindedness to how the man was speaking.

It is common among Indians to look at someone who is suffering and sacrificing and think that that person is noble and holy. Also, seeking blessings before exams is ordinary. In America, even parents who might define themselves as agnostic show up at temple before the SAT.

Being treated as holy felt dangerous, like we were risking God's anger.

The man gestured to his son. The boy, the shell of his coat squeaking, hurried to my mother. He kneeled. Did they actually believe my mother's blessing had power, or was it like how we allowed the miracle workers to try their cures?

My mother put her hands on the boy's head. She looked tired. "God give you everything you want."

The next night, a couple visited with their son. They knew us better and came to the back door.

After the test results were released, the man who had sounded simpleminded approached us at temple and thanked my mother. He did this despite the fact that his son had not done especially well.

· · ·

NEWS OF MY mother's blessings spread. There was an SAT in November, another in January, and a third in March. With each there was an increase in people coming for blessings. Some were middle-class people, and they spoke casually to my mother, as if to a friend. They were obviously only bringing their children as a form of insurance, making sure they did everything they could to take care of them. Others—those who didn't know us or were lower class—were more formal. The poorest and least educated of these would go into Birju's room and touch his pale, swollen, inward-turned feet, as if the sacrifices being made for him had turned him into an idol.

My mother continued to appear uncomfortable when asked to bless a boy or girl. She would lean back when she blessed, as if trying to be far away from what she was doing. She would also speak quickly and under her breath. Usually she borrowed the formulas that older people use at weddings. "Live a thousand years. Be healthy and happy." And this too was a way of making the blessing into something ordinary.

A few of the women who came for blessings returned regularly. They came several times a week and had tea. Sometimes, if they found milk or juice on sale, they would bring cartons of these. The women were deferential to my mother, calling her "elder sister" or using the formal, plural *you* in Hindi. My mother was formal in return, afraid, I think, of intimacy because intimacy might lead to the women spending more time in the house and learning of my father's drinking.

In my mind I called these visitors "the women with problems." They wouldn't have thought of themselves this way. Having spent most of their lives in India, where a bad marriage is often accepted as a part of life and where depression and mental illness are described as a person being moody, they saw these things as just life. Unhappy, though, and sometimes embarrassed that their lives were not as perfect as in the movies or as one was expected to pretend them to be at temple, they wanted to talk to someone. My mother, because she was considered holy, was also seen as someone who would be compassionate and whose very presence might be calming.

A woman visited us because her husband had become very religious. Mrs. Hasta was pretty. She had long hair that reached her hips and shiny white teeth. Her husband was an engineer who had recently been denied a promotion. His managers had told him that he didn't write English well.

Now, Mrs. Hasta told my mother that her husband had begun praying for an hour every morning and two hours every night. She told this to us at our kitchen table. She looked down as she spoke. "The children cry when he tells them to sit with him and pray. I told him to let them pray on their own, and so he says to them, 'If this is how you want to be, then that is the fate God has given me.' He looks at the children so angrily they cry." Because of my mother's reputation for piety, Mrs. Hasta asked her to intervene on her behalf and arranged for her husband to pay us a visit.

He arrived late one afternoon while my mother was feeding Birju his pureed fruit. Mr. Hasta had once been fat and was now skinny so the skin on his face hung loose and wrinkled. He stood at the foot of Birju's exercise bed and started an argument. "Have you read Swami Vivekananda?" he asked my mother. "What about Osho? He used to be called Rajneesh."

After he left, my mother said, "That man has such pride."

I said, "He couldn't get promoted and now he lectures us."

"Where do these idiots come from?" she spat.

We were both bruised from not being treated as special.

Several women visited because their sons were eating meat and they wanted them to be vegetarian. These women were usually lower class since middle-class people, thinking their children would be accepted into America, were more willing to let them behave like Americans. Often the visits were slightly ridiculous. Once, Mrs. Disai, short, dark skinned, oval faced, entered our kitchen walking beside her son who was sixteen or seventeen, tall, broad shouldered, muscular. There were not that many children older than I was back then. I saw Mukul and thought of Birju. I wondered why Mukul was all right and my brother wasn't, and I began resenting him.

"Confess to Shuba auntie," Mrs. Disai said, seated at the kitchen table. "Tell her everything." Mukul said nothing. He was at the head of the table. He was wearing cologne, which seemed overly glamorous. The sort of person who wore cologne was bound to have a girlfriend and so not focus on his studies. "Talk, talk," his mother said. "Reveal your shame."

"Why should I be ashamed?" he said.

"He has fallen into bad company," Mrs. Disai explained. "His friends are all Spanish. We came here before other Indians. We were here even before Mr. Narayan. We used to drive with Mr. Narayan to New York to buy groceries. Back then, the only boys who would welcome Mukul were the Spanish and the blacks."

My mother sat with her back to the window. She tried to get Mukul to change. "Why do you need to eat meat?" she asked. "Don't hens love their little chicks?"

"Look at how big you are," Mrs. Disai demanded. "You're already a buffalo."

"Gandhiji ate meat, too," my mother said, nodding and sounding understanding. "It's in his autobiography. He did it only once. You, too, can put meat in the past."

Mukul stared at the table and sighed.

"He wants to be like the blacks, like the Spanish. Why don't you get divorced? Steal? Then you will be like them. Then you'll be happy."

"Listen to your mother," my mother said. "Don't break her heart."

"Say something," Mrs. Disai shouted. "Do you have any brains? Do you want me to die?"

"You won't die," Mukul said. He had a rumbling voice. To me, he seemed too relaxed and too accepting of himself.

"And you'll live forever if you eat Chicken McNuggets?"

Mukul let out a long breath.

"Come look at what we do for you," she hissed.

The three stood up from the table and walked toward Birju's room. I had been watching quietly from near the stove. Now I hurried after because this was my time to show off.

Once the three of them were lined up by the exercise bed, I climbed on. I placed one of Birju's feet against my shoulder and began leaning forward and then rocking back. The stretching was part of Birju's physical therapy.

"This is love, animal," Mrs. Disai scolded. "And you won't do one thing for me."

Before they left, she stood in the kitchen and made her son put his hand on her head and swear not to eat meat.

Seventh grade passed and I entered eighth. It was now normal for women to come to our house and sit at the kitchen table and drink tea. Once or twice a week, whole families appeared. Usually they came after dinner. I was glad for the company, especially for those who visited at night. Often, after Birju had been fed and put back in his bed, my mother and I would sit on either side of him and my father would go upstairs to his room. Then, as my mother and I played cards, I would feel so alone that it was like we were at the bottom of an ocean.

The families that visited would talk for awhile about Birju and his health. They might discuss school or compare India and America. The problems that would lead to Indira Gandhi's assassination were taking place and sometimes people spoke of this.

I used to like listening to people speak of India. I would get excited. It was as if a part of me had begun believing that India did not actually exist, that it was a fairy tale, and having these people speak of it confirmed that it was real.

. . .

My FATHER'S DRINKING worsened. The disorder that had been restricted primarily to weekend mornings spread into the week. Sometimes my father was too hungover in the morning to bathe Birju. He would lie on his bed in his pajamas, one foot touching the floor to keep the room from spinning. When this happened, I took on his role in bathing my brother. Standing in the tub, holding Birju up, rubbing him with soap, feeling his flabby chest, his stretched stomach, I would be moved to tears that we were not better people, that my poor brother was in need and we were not as good as we should be.

My parents fought so much that the walls vibrated with rage. Anything could spark a shouting match: a banana peel left on the kitchen table, a garden hose left overnight on the lawn. The anger was so quick and extraordinary that it appeared disconnected from what was supposed to be the cause. This made the fights feel hallucinatory.

Adding to the sense of the fantastical were things that I saw and half failed to understand: my mother standing in the laundry room at two or three in the morning, shaking with rage as she put bed sheets smelling of urine into the machine. Another time, I noticed that there was a large rough patch on the pale blue carpet by my father's side of the bed. Several days later, I was sitting on the school bus when I suddenly realized that my father must have vomited on the carpet.

. . .

MY MOTHER WANTED to keep the family from embar-rassment, and so did I.

When we had visitors, my mother was modest. She listened without speaking. She tried to efface herself and let the guests lead the conversation. This hiding herself appeared smart because who knew what attention could lead to?

When visiting, people regularly asked to see my father. My mother would answer, with a downward glance, "He has great tiredness." This was a strange phrase, both formal and awkward. "Unhai bahut thakan hai." The phrase did not say that he was feeling tired but that he possessed tiredness, and with its indirection highlighted that something was being avoided and so asked the listener to not inquire further.

Usually, my mother's request was honored. Most men and women would use formal diction and say, "With a life like yours, who wouldn't be tired?" A few people pressed my mother. They threatened to go upstairs and bring my father down. "I won't take no for an answer," a woman said once. This demand to see my father was flattery. It was a way of declaring intimacy, that the woman loved us enough to make demands. This woman was, I think, a little crazy—the sort of person who loved to say the things that are uttered in mov-ies. My mother listened to the woman and gave a quick smile to acknowledge the flattery. She remained firm, though. The melodramatic woman looked at us eagerly, wanting us to engage. When my mother did not respond, the woman had to remain silent also, and then the conversation switched on its own to something else.

While these people were in the house, I tried to be very good so that none of the positive opinion they had of us because of Birju was diminished by anything I did. To make sure we were perceived well, I would rush around the house carrying cups of tea, plates of biscuits, trying to appear sweet and helpful and trying to keep the visitors distracted from thinking about my father.

Keeping him always hidden was not possible, of course. My father didn't take house keys to work. One evening, returning home, he rang the back doorbell while my mother was entertaining her friend Mrs. Sethi in the kitchen. My mother didn't hear it. When he rang again and my mother let him in, he accused her of trying to teach him a lesson. "You want to humiliate me, Shuba," he shouted. "You think you know everything and the rest of the world knows nothing."

My mother giggled with embarrassment. Mrs. Sethi, sitting at the kitchen table, looked away. She was dark skinned and curly haired and she was a kind woman. She used to take me to the mall if I needed school supplies. "All right, Grandfather." My mother said. "Why are you so upset?"

"Brother-in-law," Mrs. Sethi said, standing up, "I too would get upset if I came home from working all day and couldn't enter my house." Among the many kind people who helped my family, Mrs. Sethi always seemed one of the more socially graceful, one of those people who do not make their life worse by getting into unneeded drama.

"See how kind she is," my mother said to my father, reminding him to control himself before company.

My father glared at them, sweating.

MY FATHER ONLY fought with my mother, but my mother fought with me as well. She screamed at me if she caught me reading in the bathroom, which she considered a filthy habit. If I came home from school and did not immediately go say hello to Birju, she accused me of avoiding my brother. Once, when Birju was in his wheelchair and my father was feeding him, I happened to be walking past Birju and my brother coughed and some of the brown mush he was being fed landed on my fingers. I wiped my hand on the towel that lay over his chest.

"I saw that," my mother shouted. She was standing at the stove.

"What did you see?"

"You put snot on his towel."

"I did not. I did not!"

"I know what I saw."

I began to have the sense that my mother disliked me, that she tolerated me in the house because it was her duty.

. . .

OCCASIONALLY THERE WERE moments of kindness in the family. On my father's birthday, my mother prepared his favorite foods, and she fasted from morning till evening. And when my father got home, he showered and then all three of us went to the altar in my parents' room.

Periodically on our evening walks, my mother and I would look at houses and talk about how we might change our house: paint a large rock white and place it in the center of our front lawn, get wooden squirrels and screw them to the side of the house so that they looked like they were climbing toward the roof.

I WAS ALWAYS LOST in a book, whether I was actually reading or imagining myself as a character. If bad things happened, like Birju developing pneumonia and having to wear an oxygen mask, I would think that soon I would be able to go back to my reading and then time would vanish and when I reentered the world, the difficult thing would be gone or changed.

I often lied about my reading. The books I liked were science fiction and fantasy, books where things were not as complicated and unsatisfying as real life. I claimed to have read more famous books, though—the ones our teachers told us were for older students or the ones that had been made into movies. One winter morning in ninth grade, while it was still dark outside, I sat at our kitchen table and began reading a biography of Ernest Hemingway called *The Young Hemingway*, hoping that if I read the biography, I could then more effectively pretend to have read him. All I knew about Hemingway was that he was famous and that he was a writer.

The biography opens with Hemingway on a boat that is entering New York Harbor. The day is gray, and seagulls are soaring above him. He is returning to America from Paris and World War I. As I read about Hemingway having been to Spain and France, I was amazed. I couldn't believe that an actual person had gotten to go to Spain and France. What was even more amazing was that this man had done it without being a doctor or an engineer. Till then I had thought that the only way to have a good life was to have one of these two professions. As I sat there reading, I got happier and happier. To have a life where one traveled, where one did what one wanted, seemed like being rich.

The light outside the window turned blue. Trees and nearby houses grew visible as if they were emerging out of water. The happiness was so intense it was as if my chest were being stretched.

It took several days to finish the biography. I read it mostly at the kitchen table. As I read, I began wanting to be a writer. I had written short stories in class before. Now, I thought about how wonderful it would be to be a writer and get attention and get to travel and not have to be a doctor or an engineer. As I sat there reading, my mother came in and out of the kitchen. She opened and closed the refrigerator. She prepared meals. Fantasizing about a life which was far away from her and Birju, I felt like I was doing something dishonest.

The same day that I finished the biography, I went to the library. I asked the librarian if there were more books on Hemingway. The woman, young, pregnant, asked if I wanted books about Hemingway or by him. I felt embarrassed saying that I did not want to read his works, that I only wanted to learn how to be a writer and get famous. "About him," I murmured. She smiled and appeared pleased. I think she mistook my interest as me being scholarly. She led me to an aisle and showed me the library's ten or twelve hardbacks on Hemingway. The biographer had mentioned that Hemingway's style was very simple. I understood this to mean that if I became a writer, I wouldn't have to be very good, that being merely acceptable would be sufficient for me to have a good life. I checked out all the books.

In my bedroom, I sat on the floor behind my bed so that if anybody came in I would not be immediately seen and so, in this way, I felt hidden. I began reading the books with a mixture of hope and embarrassment. I started with the thinnest book. It was a collection of essays. I began by reading the book's introduction. Normally when I did things that appeared difficult, like connecting a VCR with a TV, I didn't read the instructions, for I was afraid of failure, and reading the directions only made me more anxious that I would fail. With learning to write, I wanted to do everything that could possibly help.

Usually it embarrassed me to read slowly, as if the amount of time I was spending proved I was stupid. This time I read each paragraph carefully. If my mind wandered in the middle, I reread the paragraph, which happened several times a page. The first essay compared physical space in Hemingway's only play, *The Fifth Column*, with physical space in the story "Hills Like White Elephants." I didn't know the play or the story. I didn't understand the terms that the essay used. The sentences were like long weeds waving from the bottom of a muddy pond. I read the essay carefully, afraid, trying to hold what I could in my head.

The second essay made no sense, either. As I read it, I felt stupid for having thought I could be a writer. Still I kept reading. Now and then I learned something that struck me as practical. One essay said that Hemingway got away with writing plainly because he wrote about exotic things. If he were to write about ordinary things in an ordinary way, he would be boring. This remark was inserted in the middle of a paragraph. Reading it, I was shocked that something so important could be hidden like this. As long as I wrote about exotic things, I thought, I could then be a not very good writer and still be successful.

Another essay said that all of Hemingway's protagonists are noble. If they were not, the lack of emotion in the prose would make them seem to be psychopaths. I thought that if I were to write, this was a clue as to what kind of characters I should write about. From an essay on ecology I learned that Hemingway often used repetition to create a physical impression, that in "Big Two-Hearted River" he described the weather as hot and then a little later he described the back of the character's neck as hot. In that same essay, the author mentioned that physical description in Hemingway's third person narratives tends to be at the start of paragraphs, while in first person narratives, physical description gets spread throughout the paragraph. Still another essay referred to how the dialogue tags "he said" and "she said" usually come at the end of a line of speech. Sometimes, though, when characters are very emotional, speech is preceded with "Henry said," or "Cathy said," and putting the label before the dialogue makes it feel stilted. This acts as a way of tamping down emotion and forces the reader to invest in trying to feel what the characters feel. Each of these things I noticed and put away. I wondered what it would be like to actually read Hemingway. Would I find it boring?

The second book I read was a slightly thicker collection of essays. Once again, I rarely understood what the writers were talking about. But now I knew a few more things. An essayist wrote that *The Old Man and the Sea* is full of factual inaccuracies, that it is impossible to carry miles of fishing line on one's shoulder. Even though I hadn't read the novel, I felt I knew the book from having read other essays. I read about Hemingway's mistakes and felt that what probably matters in a book is its emotional truth and not whether small facts are accurate. Still another essayist mentioned how Hemingway, when he wanted to make his dialogue surprising, would take speech he had assigned to one character and give it to another, that some of the dialogue spoken by the Jewish character in *The Sun Also Rises* originally belonged to the protagonist of the novel. Giving the Jewish character this dialogue made him less one-dimensional.

Reading these books I had the feeling that I was being transformed. I felt like I was being connected to a world where stories were written and where they were studied. Feeling myself being connected, I had the sense that I was being taken away from my own life and brought into a world that was glamorous, where people did pleasurable things, where people did not worry all the time.

It took me several months to read the critical books. When I was done with them, I asked my mother to take me to the mall. The B. Dalton Bookseller was on the second floor. Mostly it sold magazines, calendars, greeting cards. In the front of the store was a wall of magazines, and there were tables that offered books by the foot. Beyond this, after shelves devoted to psychology and spirituality, was a section called Literature. I went to this and looked for Hemingway. There was a shelf and a half of paperbacks. My mother stood beside me as I pulled out different titles. Her watching me made me nervous. Because she often looked to criticize me, I felt she might think I was wasting money. The books were white with black drawings of matadors and of hills and small boats. I had decided to buy them instead of checking them out of the library because I felt that spending money would force me to read them. At the cash register, my mother watched as I paid with money I had received for various birthdays. I could feel her gaze.

That night, during dinner, my mother told my father that

I had used my own money to buy books. "What an amazing boy," she said. "It's very good what you are doing, Ajay." She said this seriously.

I sat hidden on the floor behind my bed and began reading. I started with the first book that he had published. The stories bored me. When I read the one about the mules having their knees broken and being thrown off a pier in a besieged city, I felt nothing. I understood from what I had read that the plainness of the writing was supposed to let the reader form his own response. To me, though, the mules didn't feel real and neither did the pier. Till then I had only read about Hemingway—never anything by him. I had been afraid to do so because what would happen if I didn't like him? Reading the stories, I became afraid that I might have wasted all the time that I had spent with the critical essays. Surely my not liking the stories showed some failure in me.

I began to take notes as I read. Doing something while reading reduced my anxiety at not being interested. I started counting the number of words in each sentence. On top of each sentence, I wrote a 3 or 5 or 7 in blue ink. Because I knew "and" was an important word in Hemingway's sentences, I circled each "and." Every page I read became crowded with blue writing.

I started *The Sun Also Rises*. When there were stretches of dialogue and the page looked bare, I circled the "he said," "she said," or wrote "no dialogue label."

I got to the end of the first chapter and began reading it again. A quarter of the way into the book, I started to respond in the ways that I thought Hemingway had wanted his readers to react. At one point in the novel, a burly wealthy man lifts up his shirt to show scars from arrow wounds. I had read an essay about this character. Because the essay had told me what I should feel, I felt it—a sense of the two main characters of the novel being shoved to the side of the story by a character whose world is so much larger than theirs. The change in perspective was a physical sensation, like standing up suddenly and becoming light-headed and the room pulling away.

As I kept reading Hemingway, who seemed to so value suffering in silence, I began to see my family's pain as belonging in a story. In the morning, watching my father bathe Birju, I fantasized about writing how my father's pajamas grew wet and translucent until I could see through to his underwear. At the idea of writing sentences that contained our suffering, I experienced both the triumph that I had felt when I told Jeff and Michael Bu about Birju, and also a sort of detachment, like I was watching my own life.

Other things in my life, though, were too undignified and strange to be converted into literature. A housing development was being built a few blocks away, with frames of yellow two-by-fours and lawns of orange dirt. A few houses were nearly complete. These had For Sale signs before them, and their lawns were newly covered in rectangles of sod. Often, either because my father did not believe that grass could be considered property or because he did not wish to believe this, he drove to the houses and stole their grass. He tore the sod off the ground and put it into the back of our silver station wagon and brought it home. As he placed these pads all over our lawn, my mother came out and shouted at him that at least he should be smart and do this at night.

After four or five months of reading Hemingway, I decided to write a story. I had in the past written stories for English classes. These had all been about white people, because white people's stories seemed to matter more. Also, I hadn't known how to write about Indians. How would I translate the various family relations, the difference between an uncle who is a father's brother and an uncle who is a mother's brother? Having read Hemingway, I knew that I should just push all the exotic things to the side as if they didn't matter, that this was how one used exoticism—by not bothering to explain.

The first story I wrote was about my brother coughing. I woke one night to the sound of Birju coughing downstairs and then could not go back to sleep. To be woken this way and not be able to return to sleep struck me as sad enough to merit a reader's attention. Also, Hemingway had written a story about a man being woken because somebody is dying nearby, and the man is forced to witness the death.

I got up from my bed and turned on the light. I then returned to bed with a spiral-bound notebook and placed it against my knees. I began my story in the middle of the action the way Hemingway did. I wrote:

The coughing wakes me. My wife coughs and coughs, and then when her throat is clear, she moans. The nurse's aide moves back and forth downstairs. The hospital bed jingles.

I wrote that it was a spouse coughing because that seemed something a reader could identify with, while a brother would be too specific to me.

I lie here, listening to my wife cough, and it is hard to believe that she is dying.

It was strange to write something down and for that thing to come into existence. The fact that the sentence existed made Birju's coughing somehow less awful.

As I sat on my bed, I thought about how I could end my story. I held my pencil above the sheet of paper. According to the essays I had read on Hemingway, all I needed to do was attach something to the end of the story that was both unexpected and natural.

I imagined Birju dying; this had to be what would eventually happen. As soon as I imagined this, I did not want him gone. I felt a surge of love for Birju. Even though he was sick and swollen, I did not want him gone. I wrote:

I lie in my bed and listen to her cough and am glad she is coughing because this means she is alive. Soon she will die, and I will no longer be among the lucky people whose wives are sick. Fortunate are the men

*whose wives cough. Fortunate are the men who cannot sleep through
the night because their wives' coughing wakes them.*

Writing the story changed me. Now I began to feel as if I
were walking through my life collecting things that could be
used later: the sound of a Ping-Pong ball was like a woman
walking in high heels, the shower running was like television static. Seeing things as material for writing protected
me. When a boy tried to start a fight by saying, "You're vegetarian—does that mean you don't eat pussy?" I thought this
would be something I could use in a story.

At the end of ninth grade, as I was about to turn fifteen, I and ten other students had straight As. This meant that we were all ranked first in our class.

The day school ended, there was a carnival atmosphere. Students emptied their lockers into the hallways, throwing papers, magazine cutouts, and greeting cards all over the floors. In each classroom a sheet of paper was pinned to the bulletin board and typed on this were the names of those ranked first in their grade. Seeing my name in type made it feel like another person's.

When I came home, my mother was exercising Birju, moving his arms up and down as if he were marching.

"Mommy," I said, my hand on Birju's foot because by showing respect I could make myself younger, "I'm ranked first in my class."

"Very good," my mother answered, continuing to pump Birju's arms.

She didn't say any more. I had been feeling proud as well as guilty, and now I felt a collapse. And then I became disgusted with myself for my vanity in wanting to be thought special when ten other children were also ranked first.

Pᴇᴏᴘʟᴇ ᴘʜᴏɴᴇᴅ ᴀɴᴅ asked my mother if I could speak to their children. I remembered how the same thing had happened when Birju got into the Bronx High School of Science. I remembered my jealousy then. Now, talking on the phone to those children, it seemed to me that to be one among eleven students was nothing compared to Birju getting into his school after only a year and a half in America.

My mother and I began to be invited to people's houses so that their children could see me and realize that boys who were ranked first looked and sounded like anybody else.

One night, I sat between two girls, six and ten, at a dining-room table. My mother and the girls' parents, both doctors, sat across from me. I spoke and spoke. I remembered how my father had talked when we sat in Mr. Gupta's Mercedes.

"For Indians, it is important to do well in English. There are so many of us who do well in math that colleges don't pay math and science much attention."

The mother of the girls asked, "These teachers—they don't favor their own?" She said this in Hindi, as if this fear of favoritism, which was a reasonable one in India, prompted her to speak like she was still there.

Her husband asked whether I played Atari and whether I

thought it was worth buying a computer. "A typewriter is all one needs," I said. Like his wife, the man also spoke timidly. I found it strange that two doctors could have fears.

A few of the men we visited appeared to see me as competition. One man twisted my earlobe and said, "So, genius, you are very smart." Another man had me sit on a white sofa while he sat on a white easy chair at a right angle from me. Then, he tested me on how much I knew. He asked what words "percent" was a contraction of and how many elements were on the periodic table.

I felt important because of my class rank. Soon after tenth grade started, I tried getting a girlfriend.

Rita was five foot three. She had thick eyebrows, a heart-shaped face, and wavy hair that fell to her shoulders. She spoke without an accent. This and the fact that she sat with white girls at lunch placed her in a better world than mine.

One afternoon I phoned her from my parents' room. I paced by my parents' bed, the phone to my ear. My mother had just prayed, and there was an incense stick smoking on the altar. The phone began to ring on the other end.

"Hello?" a girl said.

"Is Rita there?" I asked. I stood looking out a window. Outside, the trees were changing color.

"Yes. Hold on. Who's this?"

"Ajay."

"Ajay from Morristown?"

"From school."

"Rita," the girl screamed.

A moment later, there was an echo as an extension was lifted.

"Who's this?" another girl said.

I thought this was Rita but wasn't sure. "Rita?"

"Yes."

"It's Ajay."

"Ajay from Morristown?"

"No. From school."

"Ajay?"

"We're in math class together."

"OK."

There was silence. I had decided to tell Rita I loved her. This was because from having watched Hindi movies, it seemed that if one was to have a relationship with a girl, one had to be in love. Also, it seemed easier to say I loved her than to have a conversation. "I think you're very beautiful," I said.

Rita didn't reply. I became silent again. I stared out the picture window above my parents' bed. Our backyard ran into another, and this second yard into a third, and the leaves of the trees were gold and orange.

"You are the most beautiful girl in school." My face and neck were burning.

"Thank you."

"Would you like to go on a date?"

Rita was silent for a moment.

"With you?"

"Yes."

"No."

I began to make excuses for having called. "I only asked because I thought you didn't have a boyfriend."

Suddenly Rita shrieked, "Are you on the phone?"

"Yes," I murmured.

"Get off. Get off."

I heard the "huh, huh, huh" of somebody laughing.

"Get off."

I wanted to hang up. "I love you." I felt somehow obligated to say this.

"Huh, huh, huh," went the other person on the line.

"I'll call you back," Rita said.

"Do you need my phone number?"

She hung up.

For a few days I was embarrassed. The first time I entered math class after the call, I saw Rita and my entire back became hot.

I KNEW ENOUGH ABOUT myself to realize that I had to immediately try again with another girl. If I didn't, I would seize up with shyness. With this second girl, I tried not to be too ambitious.

Minakshi was not pretty. She was shorter than Rita and

had a worried, pinched face. When she walked down the school's hallways, she kept both straps of her book bag over her shoulders, and she hunched forward as if carrying a heavy burden. Minakshi's father owned a television repair shop and said that he was an engineer, though my father said that it was obvious that he had not even finished high school. Right after we brought Birju from the nursing home, Mr. Nair had suggested we transport Birju to his house and try dipping him into his swimming pool. Mr. Nair was very conservative. My mother had once volunteered my father to drive Minakshi and her sisters somewhere, and Mrs. Nair had said her husband did not like men who were not relatives to be alone with their daughters.

One afternoon, Minakshi was walking down a set of the school's stairs. She was holding a binder across her chest and she looked pained, as she often did. I was climbing the stairs. There were boys and girls around us and their footsteps and voices made the stairwell loud. Passing her, I said, "I love you." I said this in an ordinary conversational voice. Minakshi continued down the stairs. She seemed not to have heard.

A few days later, she was kneeling by her locker, a forest of jean-clad legs around her. I went up to her and, walking swiftly, dropped a scrap of paper in her hair. She grabbed the top of her head, looking angry, like someone used to being treated badly. I remembered being spat on while crouched before my locker. The note said, "I love you."

For a while I continued trying to hide myself when I told

Minakshi I loved her. We were in the same gym class. Running past her in her big, baggy shorts, banging a basketball against the floor, I whispered, "I love you." Sometimes she appeared to have heard me. She would look around open mouthed.

Telling Minakshi I loved her, slipping notes through the grill of her locker door, was like taking part in an adventure. I also, though, regularly blamed Minakshi for the nervousness I was experiencing from telling her I loved her.

About a week after I started doing this, I was walking down a hallway and she was walking toward me. The hallway was crowded and noisy. There were voices and locker doors slamming and rattling. I was thinking about whether it was possible to drift across the hall toward Minakshi, whisper my love, and disappear without being noticed.

Minakshi saw me and stopped. I came near her. We were two or three feet apart. She was wearing a shiny pink blouse. "Ajay," she said. I stopped. She crossed over toward me. She looked hurt. "Are you the one telling me you love me?"

I worried she might tell her parents, who would then inform my mother. I was afraid, though, of passing up the opportunity of getting a girlfriend. "Yes."

"OK. We can talk after school." She walked away.

Immediately I felt regret. To me, all relationships were serious and full of obligations, and the idea of having one suddenly felt like a burden.

At the end of the day, Minakshi and I met outside our

school's doors. Yellow buses lined the horseshoe driveway. We walked up toward the road. At first we didn't talk. My mouth was dry. When we reached the road, we turned right, in the direction of where she lived. The sidewalk went up a slope. Both of us were bent under our book bags.

A part of me was still afraid that Minakshi was going to threaten to tell her mother. I had known boys who had approached girls, and the girls had done so.

Minakshi, not looking at me, said, "My father won't let me receive phone calls."

This seemed to imply that she was open to being my girl-friend. I was relieved. "My parents don't like me getting calls either. Except from boys."

"I don't want anyone to know I have a boyfriend. Some-body might tell my mother just to cause trouble."

"Me, too. People gossip."

"Studies come first."

I nodded quickly. "For me also. Marriage and love can come when studies are done and one is established in one's profession."

"We can talk," Minakshi said.

"But only if we are alone and nobody can overhear."

"I don't want sex until I'm married."

"I don't want to kiss." Raising the standards of what was proper was a way of making myself more appealing, more trustworthy.

We stopped talking. The air was cold and smelled of moist

earth, and this seemed wonderful. We came to a street corner and crossed. On the other side, Minakshi said, "If you had a dog, what would you name it?"

In the past, when I had thought about having a dog, I had imagined that possessing one would make me white, like one of those boys on TV who hugged their pet when unhappy. I had given this dog an American-type name like Scout or Goldie. Now, imagining a dog within the context of having a girlfriend, it seemed disloyal to give the dog a white dog's name, as if then I would be giving affection to a white dog instead of an Indian one, and so would not be acting adult and proper. "Something Indian," I said.

"Me, too."

Minakshi became silent. The road we were on began to curve away. After a moment, Minakshi said, "I'll be your girlfriend."

"Good," I said and stopped. "I have to turn back."

"Don't call me," she said. "My parents will get upset."

"OK. I won't. You don't call either."

WITHIN A FEW weeks Minakshi and I were kissing. When I tried to get us to start doing this, I wasn't sure how to suggest it without appearing like I was going back on my word. I therefore pouted and hinted vaguely at Birju being sick so Minakshi would try comforting me.

Behind our school was a football field bordered by a track. Beyond this were woods. The woods, mostly maples and crab apples, were where students who did not have places to make out went. Minakshi and I walked into the woods one afternoon. The day was very cold and the fallen leaves reached our ankles. When we had gone far enough for the school between the trees to look distant, we stopped.

I was excited to kiss for the first time. I also felt that I was taking advantage of Minakshi. To me, it seemed that the only reason she was coming into the woods with me was because she was trying to soothe me, that she felt no desire of her own.

Minakshi was wearing a long blue parka that came to her knees. I was wearing a blue ski jacket. We hugged. Our coats squeaked. My heart was racing. I brought my face down to hers. The warmth of her body, the smell of spices from what she ate surprised me. She felt real and mysterious in a way that took me aback.

I believed that proper kissing required not breathing on the person one was kissing. We kissed and kissed. I held my breath. Blue sparks floated before me.

School ended at 2:35, and the nurse's aide left at four. I had to get back before then. I walked home. The sky looked somehow new. I was so happy that my pace kept speeding up. I had the feeling that everything would be OK for me, that one day everything would be fine.

Birju was lying on his exercise bed beneath the chandelier. Seeing him, I remembered our apartment in Queens, how the intercom would ring when his girlfriend was downstairs. I remembered Nancy's long black hair. I wondered what had happened to her.

MINAKSHI AND I kissed every day. Once, it was raining and I didn't think we could go out, and she said, "I have an umbrella." When she said this, I thought I had misheard her. The fact that she, too, wanted to kiss was hard to believe.

I had meant to be like Amitabh Bachchan with Minakshi— silent, mysterious. I found, though, that I could not stop talking, that when we were in the woods and I would pull away from her to breathe, I would immediately start speaking, that I wanted to talk as much as I wanted to kiss.

At first I said the sorts of things that would stir up pity or portray me as brave. I told her about how smart Birju had been. I told her how I bathed him in the morning and how, often, after we put him back into his hospital bed, Birju, warm and relaxed, tended to piss on himself. After a little while, though, I began telling her things which were so awful that I had somehow managed not to acknowledge them.

When Birju had gotten pneumonia, he had had a series of

convulsions. These had caused more brain damage. Before the convulsions, if there was a loud noise, he would swing his head in the direction of the noise. Now when there was a noise, he wouldn't react—he'd remain smacking his lips and looking lost in thought. Earlier Birju had been able to sit mostly straight in his wheelchair. Now, when we sat him up, he began slumping. To keep him upright, we had to put his arms through a vest of sorts. The vest was missing a back but had long straps on the sides. We used these to tie Birju to his wheelchair.

I did not normally spend money on the vending machines in school. Spending money made me anxious. After I told Minakshi about this additional brain damage, I went back into the building and bought an ice cream. I think telling her was like releasing some enormous stress and the ice cream was like how one sits down after a shock.

I found myself falling in love. Minakshi seemed kind and wonderful. Her small body, how I could gather it up in my arms like a bouquet, seemed the most extraordinary thing in the world. Loving her, I was scared. There were certain things I didn't tell her because they were humiliating—my father's drinking, my mother's irrationality and meanness. I expected to be judged based on my family, and not telling her about my parents, I felt as if I were pretending to be better than I was.

· · ·

SOMETIMES, COMING HOME from kissing Minakshi, I would see Birju on his exercise bed and get upset. I couldn't understand why everything wasn't better. I wanted to hurt someone or something. The only thing I could find to hurt was my relationship with Minakshi.

Priya was taller than I was and very skinny and had a nose like a beak. We were in biology class together, and I had spoken to her only a few times. I knew, though, that her father was a doctor and she was very smart. Also, she sat with Rita and the white girls.

I began telling Priya I loved her. Passing her on the staircase, I whispered this. I slipped little strips of paper into her locker. On the strips I wrote poems. I did this four or five times, and then Priya came up to me in biology class. I was standing in the back alongside the bulletin boards.

"Did you write this?" she asked, holding out one of the strips.

The class had not yet begun, but most of the students were already there. I was conscious of their presence. I thought of Minakshi finding out.

"No," I said.

Priya laughed. "I heard you told Rita you loved her."

I didn't say anything.

ometimes on weekends my parents went to temple or a prayer ceremony and were away for the afternoon. Minakshi came over then. First she would stand in Birju's room and say hello to him. When she did this, she looked serious. Afterward we went upstairs. We would lie on my bed fully clothed. We would kiss and rub against each other. I couldn't believe I was getting to do something so wonderful.

Minakshi seemed the embodiment of a future. The possibility of escape made me more impatient with my mother instead of less. She and I were now bathing Birju most mornings. Nearly always we fought as we did this. One morning in Birju's room, perhaps inspired by how eunuchs in India show up at people's houses and demand money and begin taking off their clothes to show they will do anything unless they are paid, I started stripping. I had just finished bathing my brother, cleaning his ass with a bar of soap, and my mother had been telling me that she knew I hated him, that whatever I did for him I did because of guilt and not because of love.

"Why should I have any shame?" I shouted once I was naked.

My mother was near the foot of the bed, embracing a folded towel. She looked at me stunned. This pleased me. We often sought to show that there was no limit to what we would say or do.

After a moment, my mother wagged her head from side to side. "If Birju were all right, I would tell you to get out. I'd tell you to leave right now. Go with your stupid grades and die."

I was not going to let her have the last word. "How can they be stupid when they're so high?"

WHILE MY FATHER'S drinking was getting so bad that he hardly helped and my mother and I were fighting every day, my family was also becoming more and more famous. This was not only because my good grades had brought another level of attention to us, but also because the community was growing and so there were simply more people to give attention.

A large apartment complex, a row of brown brick buildings called Hilltop Apartments, had opened along a wide, busy road about a mile away. Almost all of the people who lived in Hilltop were Indians, new arrivals. Riding on the school bus, I often saw them walking along the sides of roads because they didn't have cars. At temple, the women from

Hilltop, women who worked at Kmart and grocery stores, carried see-through plastic purses. These people began visiting us. Many of them spoke neither Hindi nor English. When they came, they brought coconuts and bananas as if they were visiting an actual temple. Usually they said nothing or only the few words of Hindi that they knew: namaste, beta, khush. Some of the women came into Birju's room, gripped his feet with both hands, and bowed and touched their foreheads to his feet.

My father was now drinking all night long. Many nights, I woke at three or four in the morning from hearing him coming down the hallway. The upstairs bathroom was next to my room. My father kept a bottle of scotch beneath the bathroom sink. If the creaking of the hallway floor didn't wake me, the buzz of the fluorescent tube light turning on did.

The wood of the bathroom door was swollen. One night, I heard the door being pulled close. I lay in bed and, unable to go back to sleep, became enraged.

I left my room and came out into the dark hallway. A line of white light shone beneath the bathroom door. I wanted to shout at my father. I knocked. "Who?" my father said in a slurred voice.

"Can I come in?"

I pushed the door. My father was standing by the window. He was wearing gray pajamas. His face was sagging, and his eyes were dilated. The window was open, and a moist spring breeze was blowing in.

There was something about the reality of seeing my father's loose face that made me stop being angry. "How are you, Daddy?" I asked.

"I am so happy," he answered. He was smiling.

ANOTHER MORNING I woke to the sound of my mother's voice shouting with what sounded like alarm, and I hurried to my parents' room.

"You are going to lose your job," my mother cried. She was standing at the foot of the bed while my father lay before her.

"They're all like me, Shuba," he slurred. "It's a government office."

"We won't have insurance! Birju will be thrown out on the street."

"I'm union. They say, 'Come to a meeting.' I answer, 'Is there food? I only go to meetings with food.'"

My father was almost always late for work. Sometimes he left the house at noon. Sometimes he missed a day. Coming home from school, I would see his station wagon in the driveway, and my chest would tighten. I would walk into Birju's room, see my mother sitting by the exercise bed reading to Birju, and her face would be grim. I would keep to myself, then, because I didn't want her shouting at me. I'd go upstairs to my room and sit at my desk and read Hemingway. Hemingway had been an alcoholic and his characters often drank too much. Their drinking appeared false, though, because there were no consequences. It was like how cartoon characters fall off cliffs without being injured. Spotting this lie in Hemingway made me feel superior to him, and this bit of superiority led me to feel anger and contempt and being angry was pleasurable.

At some point, my father began missing one or two days of work a week. He was put on probation. He told my mother that he sat in an office with his supervisor, his union representative, and a very fat man who was the human resources person. He signed a piece of paper to document that he had been notified of the complaint.

When he had signed the paper, his supervisor said, "I don't care if you show up drunk. You just have to come to work."

"That's not what he means," the fat man murmured.

My father was not going to be told what to do. "You want to show you have power," he shouted at his supervisor. "I know you."

When she heard this, my mother said, "They do have power."

"I am not going to be a slave, Shuba. Not for you. Not for Birju."

"Always you find a way to bring in Birju."

A few days later, I came home from school, and my father was sitting at the kitchen table. He had his back to the window. He was trying to drink tea. His hands were shaking.

My mother stood by the table. "Your father is going to

stop drinking." I wondered if I was expected to pretend to believe this. We went to Birju's room. Birju had thick acne on his cheeks now as a side effect of one of his medications. The acne was as thick as bubbled paint, but because one was not expecting it, at first glance, he appeared to have rosy cheeks.

My father put a hand on Birju's head. He swore on Birju's life that he would not drink. I saw this and thought I was watching some melodrama that my parents had concocted.

"We have to help him," my mother said to me. She said that my father was able to not drink on his own during the day. At night, though, the desire to drink was too much. He could not sleep without drinking.

That night, after Birju had received his oral feeding, the three of us sat around his hospital bed playing cards until the nurse's aide came. When my father climbed the stairs, my mother and I followed. My mother carried a thermos of tea, and I held a tray before me. The tray was covered in plates of biscuits and sweets and bowls of nuts and various types of salty fried dough.

In the bedroom, my mother flipped on the light switch by the door. She turned on the lamps that stood on the night-stands. The room became bright. There was a mirror on top of the dresser, and our reflection in this and the reflections in the windows made the room seem crowded. Pointing the remote control, she flicked on the TV. The noise added to the sense of busyness.

We sat on my parents' bed and played cards with the plates spread around us. My father sat cross-legged, head bowed, looking hopeless.

My mother asked me about school.

"It will be harder to be ranked first this year than last," I said, angry that I was being asked to engage in this foolishness.

"Already making excuses."

"It will be harder. Each year, it's harder."

The hours passed. Around two that night, my mother got tired. She turned to my father. "Do you feel sleepy?"

"No."

She put a videotape in the VCR. I cleared the bed of plates and cups. We turned off the lights and lay stretched on the bed, my father in the middle. The television shook its light over us.

My father didn't drink that night. The next evening, around five, he called to say that he was leaving work and should be home by six. The fact that my father made sure he told us this seemed to indicate that he was trying not to drink.

This second night, too, I sat with my mother and father by Birju's bed. And then at ten, we marched up the stairs with the tea and snacks.

Two days passed without drinking and then three. I began feeling a strange exhilaration. At school I would picture us going up the stairs with my father. I would look forward to this.

· · ·

For several months, my father did not drink. In my memory, this period is wonderful. Tenth grade ended, and I was again ranked first. Summer started. I turned sixteen. During those months, I was so happy that at night I had a hard time sleeping. I would be asleep, yet I would be aware of my happiness the way that, when you sleep in a room full of sun, you are aware of the light.

When he came home from work, my father was quiet, glum. Sometimes he would go upstairs to change his clothes and not come down. I would go get him, and he would be sitting at the edge of his bed looking overwhelmed. The only time my father was his old self was when he was fighting with my mother. "You don't care. You think you know what's right and that everybody else is a fool." Still, the fighting was much less than it used to be, and in my view, my mother was very patient. When my father shouted at her, she listened and did not reply. Once, she told him that what he was doing was very difficult and that every day she prayed he had strength.

I was glad for our changed life. In the morning, my father descended the stairs to bathe Birju. At night, my parents no longer shouted so loudly that the nurse's aide had to come and stand at the bottom of the stairs and call out, "Mrs. Mishra, Mrs. Mishra," in a high, put-upon voice.

I continued worrying that my father would drink. When he got home and went up the stairs, I watched to see if he put his hand on the railing, because he used to do this for support when he was drunk. At night, if I heard the swollen bathroom door shoved shut, I would wake and lie there, even though I had checked and there was no bottle of scotch under the sink.

One evening in the fall, 6:00 p.m. arrived and my father's silver station wagon did not swing into the driveway. My mother and I went to Birju's room and hefted him into his wheelchair. I rolled him into the kitchen. I stood the wheelchair at the head of the table and began feeding him pureed roti and lentils.

Seven passed. "What's happened to him?" my mother asked nervously, wiping down the counters with tight looping motions.

We rolled Birju back to his bed. The television was on. We laid him down and sat on either side of him and played cards. Birju puffed spit and rolled his blind eyes.

My father came home around nine. My mother and I stood by the living room window and watched the car enter our driveway. She, always worried about my father being drunk in public, said, "Thank God the aide isn't here."

In the kitchen a little later, my mother pleaded with my father. "This happens. Nobody can be perfect forever. Once or twice you make mistakes."

My father was standing by the sink, his face dark and flushed. "Stop bothering me," he murmured.

"Will you eat? Eat something."

"Leave me alone."

For a week, my father kept away from alcohol. He restrained himself without our having to stay awake beside him through the night.

He started drinking after this week and then, everything was exactly as it had been: him lying on the side of his bed, his foot on the floor; my mother standing by him and shouting; me grabbing him and yanking him and demanding he stand. Sometimes I couldn't believe that there had been a time when he had not been drinking. In my memory, the summer that had just passed seemed long gone.

In eleventh grade, I took the PSAT. I met with my guidance counselor for help on deciding between various colleges.

Periodically Minakshi and I went to the movies. We would arrive separately, telling our parents that we were meeting friends. Being happy, I looked down on my parents for their unhappiness. I blamed them for it the way the rich cannot help but think that poor people must bring their poverty on themselves.

At home there were endless new humiliations: my father in Birju's room late at night, drunk and sitting at the edge of the

small circle of light cast by a table lamp, a Haitian aide looking at him as he talked about how happy he was.

My father loved drinking. Later he would tell me that drinking was freedom, peace of mind, that he felt like he was surrounded by problems and when he drank, it was as if the alcohol
plucked him out from among them. He once said that he would
get angry that he didn't weigh more, because if he were heavier
he would be able to drink larger quantities before passing out.
Also, he told me that it was around when he started drinking
again that he realized that he could not stop drinking, that he
had no choice in his drinking, that when he brought the bottle of scotch to his mouth, his hand would keep pressing it to
his lips even after he wanted to stop drinking. He said that he
would feel as if the hand belonged to someone else.

To be hungover all the time was awful. He said that in the
morning he would be in his car driving to the train station
and, when he heard people on the radio, it was as if they were
broadcasting from another country, that he was in a country
where there was a war going on and these people were broadcasting from a nation that was at peace.

One night, while drinking in the bathroom, my father suddenly became captivated by the romance of standing outside
in the snow in the backyard. He went downstairs, walked
outside, and stood under the quiet stars. There was a two-
inch layer of snow, and he was wearing rubber slippers. The
snow did not bother him, he later told us. He felt very proud
standing there. He thought about how far he had come. In

India he had never seen snow and neither had his father or grandfather, and now he was living in a country where it snowed every year.

After standing in the snow for a little while, my father decided to sit down. He did so. His buttocks felt cold for a moment, and then they were OK.

THE NURSE'S AIDE woke us. "Mrs. Mishra," she called from the bottom of the stairs. I woke and lay on my side and heard a mumble of voices as my mother and the woman talked.

My father had left the back door open. The aide had gone into the kitchen to get a half-full open can of Isocal formula from the fridge.

"You could have died," my mother said, rubbing my father's back with a towel as he sat on their bed in his underwear, his feet in a pail of warm water.

A month went by. My father kept drinking. One night, he did not come home.

"He could have fallen asleep on the train," I said. My mother and I were in the living room looking out at the empty driveway.

"What kind of life is this?"

Ten came, and the car that pulled into the driveway was the aide's. By eleven, I knew that something was very wrong.

I sat in my room, my back to the wall, and wrote about a man who is waiting at home for his alcoholic wife and who hates himself because he is scared and feels he can't be as angry as he wants to be. As I wrote, I felt proud at my toughness for taking whatever was happening to me and turning it into something else.

Around one, my mother came into my room. I was still writing. "Ajay, let's go to the train station." I got out of bed without saying anything. I thought I could include this trip to the station in my story.

The train station parking lot was vast and mostly empty. Every twelve parking spaces there stood a tall light. My mother and I drove up and down the rows. Sitting by my mother, I felt such overwhelming shame that when cars passed by on a nearby road, I worried that the drivers of these cars might see us and wonder what we were doing. I thought this response would be a good detail to put in my story.

The station wagon was parked facing the road. We pulled up behind it. My mother got out and walked around the car. Periodically she brought her face to one of the windows and peered inside.

AROUND NOON THE next day, the phone rang. It was my father. He had checked himself into Bellevue Hospital, on the East Side of Manhattan.

After we signed ourselves in at the hospital's front desk, my mother and I used a photocopied map to guide ourselves through the long halls, across the lobbies of what had once been separate buildings. The lobbies resembled empty marble lagoons or, if there were chairs there, waiting areas in airports.

We came to a white metal door. Next to this, on the wall, was a small button with a sign beside it: Press for Admittance. My mother pushed it.

A moment later, through a window in the door, we saw a Chinese woman in a nurse's uniform approach. The door swung open, and the nurse, who was my mother's height, was smiling and cheerful. She led us in.

As we walked past offices, she said, "Your husband is very excited to see you. Did you bring any soda?"

"No," my mother answered.

"Some of the patients are diabetic, and so we don't let soda in."

At the end of the corridor was a banner of colorful Chinese characters. As we reached the banner, I saw a man in blue pajamas walking toward us. There was something funny about the pajamas. They were stiff. The man had on an undershirt beneath the blue pajama top. I suddenly realized that the pajamas were made of paper. I was examining them when I realized the man was my father. He was smiling. I became frightened at not having recognized him. To not have recognized him made me feel like I had lost him.

"I'm glad you came," he said. "Do you want coffee?" He kept smiling. His eyes were warm and he looked excited.

My mother began crying.

My father started leading us away from the hall that we had come down. The nurse stayed behind. "I'll explain. The news is good. I'm so glad you came."

We arrived at a doorway on the right. My father pushed open the door. He kept talking and smiling. "I checked myself in yesterday. I need help, Shuba. My insurance is wonderful. I could be here for a month and it would cost only four hundred and fifty dollars."

The door opened into a lounge that smelled of burnt coffee. It had three round tables with chairs around them. One of the tables was occupied by a young Chinese woman arguing loudly in Chinese with a small gray-haired couple that looked like her parents. There was a TV bolted to the corner of the ceiling playing *Soul Train*.

My father led us to an empty table. We seated ourselves. Once we were sitting, my father turned toward me. "Most of the people here are Chinese. This is the Chinese ward."

As he spoke, I had the sense that one day I would look back on this moment and think that until then, everything was fine.

"Is there an Indian ward?"

"No."

"Why do they have a Chinese ward?"

"There are a lot of Chinese in New York."

My father glanced at my mother. "Do you want coffee?"

Looking at her lap, holding a handkerchief to her nose, she shook her head no.

My father turned back to me. "I have to stay here for a month," he said. "This is good. The longer I stay, the better." I understood that he was saying these things for my mother to hear.

"There are good doctors here," he said. "The nurses are very good. This is a common problem, this drinking thing." He was smiling and speaking confidently, and to me, this confidence made him seem delusional, like someone confidently saying things that are obviously untrue. "All the time people come into this hospital and stop drinking."

I looked at my father's eager face and felt full of love. I wanted to kiss him. He had a hand on one of his knees, and I wanted to take it and kiss it.

"In one month I will be better," he said.

My mother kept her head down, her hands over her face.

My father said, "I have doctors. I have psychologists. These Americans are experts. They know A to Z."

I examined his face. He was smiling. The more he spoke, the more I had the sense that I was losing him, that he was somehow fading away right before me.

My mother and I took the train to New York several times a week. Passing through the marshes covered in snow, I would have an aching sense of nostalgia. I was convinced that things would get worse and that one day I would look back on this period with longing.

My father's room had green walls and smelled of sweat and unwashed clothes. On the floor, inside the doorway and leading into the room, was a wide dark streak. When we visited him, I liked the door to be closed, for us to be hidden. My mother appeared to feel the same way. We would close the door and still speak softly, shyly.

During these days, I realized how much my mother cared for my father. Once, as he lay in bed, she sat beside him, her chin on her fist, and looked at him so intently that she seemed to be memorizing him. This image of love stayed with me for days. It flickered inside me like a shiny bit of glass flashing from the bottom of a stream.

There were group counseling sessions for addicts and their

families. These were in the main section of Bellevue and not in the Chinese ward. The Chinese ward, I learned, was for the mentally ill. The first session I went to was in a lounge that had maybe thirty people. Most of these were milling around in the back near the coffee pots and the powdered milk. About half of them were in blue paper pajamas. Some of the patients were seated and were so medicated they appeared to be dozing. The family members looked tired, unhappy. Unlike the patients, they didn't talk to each other. My parents and I sat to the side of the room, our backs to a window. Everybody except for us and one Chinese man and his wife was white or black or Hispanic. I was embarrassed to be the same as these people. The counselor, a short, broad-shouldered black man with a beard and a knit hat, called out, "Brothers, sisters, we're going to start."

He stood in the front of the room and spoke in a lolling accented voice for ten or fifteen minutes about how addiction was a disease. He said that one could not be cured of it, that one could not drink alcohol for thirty years and that if one began doing so again, it would be like the day one had stopped. He said that addiction was a danger against which one had to always be on guard. My father kept nodding. He had said all this and also said that now that he knew these things, he was going to be fine.

To me, it seemed very American to call drinking a disease and therefore avoid responsibility.

"Hungry, angry, lonely, tired. HALT. Watch out for these.

But an addict will use when he is happy. He'll use when he is down."

The counselor finished speaking. He invited people from the audience to talk.

Mostly it was the alcoholics who raised their hands. A young woman spoke up. She was almost crying. "I came in on Tuesday and I don't remember anything till yesterday. I don't remember. What happened? Nobody will tell me. What happened?" Her voice rose. "I am diabetic. I didn't have my medicine. I don't remember, and nobody will tell me."

Some of the alcoholics who spoke appeared to like the sound of their own voices. An elderly black man with gray hair said, "Every bottle should come with a warning: 'This bottle may cause you to lose your job. This bottle may cause you to get a divorce. This bottle may cause you to become homeless.'" He nodded in a pleased way at his own words. "I am sixty-four, and I know what day they serve cauliflower at St. Luke's, what day Bellevue has apple pie, what day ACI has turkey breast." The man was wearing paper booties with the front part scissored open, and his toenails, which were thick and black, curved over his toes.

My mother and I sat quietly watching, my mother holding a brown purse in her lap. To me, the confidence of the alcoholics was like the confidence that my father had shown when he said he would be all right.

Some of the wives and husbands spoke. They were quieter and more thoughtful than the alcoholics. A white woman said, "I know that I have to look after myself and my children, but what do I do? I don't want him to die." The man she was sitting next to, young, black, and gaunt, was leaning forward in his chair and looking down. He had a rubber band on one wrist that he kept snapping.

MY FATHER WAS released.

On the train home, my mother and I sat facing him. It was late afternoon. He was bundled in his winter coat with his gray cap pulled over his ears. He looked small and nervous. I felt anxious. At the hospital we had known he wouldn't drink. Now, I imagined that back home, he would not drink for a little while but then start again. Looking at my father's face, I had a sudden fantasy of being in Bombay, in an apartment overlooking the sea. I had only seen Bombay in the movies, and I think the fantasy came from wanting a different life.

We arrived at Metropark Station. My mother drove us home.

In the car, my father sat up front and peered out the window. The sun was bright, and we drove past houses standing behind lawns in winter light. The houses didn't look real. They resembled a set on a stage.

We entered our house through the laundry room. My father said, "I don't want to see him today. Is that all right?"

"Of course. Go upstairs. Rest."

My father left. My mother and I went to Birju's room. He was snoring, and the aide was seated beside him knitting a sweater. My mother kissed Birju and spoke to him in a childish voice.

That evening, my father got ready to go to an Alcoholics Anonymous meeting, and so did I. My mother wanted me to accompany him so that he would not go somewhere and start drinking.

The church was around the corner from us, a white, steepled building with a parking lot and a small graveyard. Inside were fifty or sixty men and women standing around talking. Some of them were smoking. There were a half dozen women with infants and toddlers. There were also a few children who were ten or eleven, whose parents, I imagined, had been unable to get babysitters. All of the people were white. They appeared strangely ordinary to me, not like people with problems.

The meeting began. People sat down in rows of chairs. There was a table near the front of the room. A man sitting at the table asked if anyone was at an AA meeting for the first time. My father raised his hand. We were in the room's back and there was a stir of excitement. People turned to look at us. I remembered the boys at school who made fun of what I brought for lunch. I hated these people who were staring. I felt that they had no manners.

A very heavy woman was also sitting at the front table. She was blond and missing teeth, and she had a two-liter bottle of

Coca-Cola on the table before her. She was the first to speak. She told her story. She said that she had started drinking when she was in fifth grade. "I would come home and have a shot of whiskey and one of my mother's Marlboros, and that's how I took the edge off." She laughed huskily. Phlegm popped in her lungs.

My father sat leaning forward, focused.

The woman talked about dropping out of school, getting married, having abortions. When she mentioned abortions, a part of me flinched. I was surprised that she would say something like this out loud.

The woman talked about her husband beating her, about how one night, he sat at the kitchen table of their house with a revolver and waited for the police to enter so he could start shooting. "I knew that was bad." The crowd laughed. I thought, *Why are you laughing at this misery? You have created trouble for everyone and now you are laughing.* "I went out the back door to tell the police my husband had a gun and was waiting inside." Then she spoke of waking up passed out in front of her son, and this, for some reason, changed things. "My life in sobriety hasn't been good. I am morbidly obese. I don't have any money. My son would like a guitar for his fourteenth birthday, and I can't buy him one. Maybe I'll ask his grandmother. She's willing to give me money now."

After this, many other people spoke. Most talked for a shorter time than the woman with the Coke. Another woman said she had recently begun drinking mouthwash. "My son is getting married, and I'm a fat pig." A man spoke about being separated from his wife and when he wanted to send his son a birthday card, he had to write the card in front of his probation officer because he wasn't allowed to have any contact with his children. I couldn't understand what most of this had to do with drinking.

I also got angrier and angrier at the thought that white people behaved in such ways and yet they were the ones who were important.

The meeting started at seven and ended at eight. When it finished, people stood around the room and held hands and said the Lord's Prayer. My father and I joined in the hand-holding and tried repeating the words as they were spoken. Saying them, I felt that we were trying to pass as whites.

Immediately after this, we were surrounded by men who began giving my father scraps of paper with their phone numbers. I wondered what these people wanted from us. At the hospital, a nurse had brought us tubes of hand lotion and bottles of talcum powder and tried to get us to convert to Christianity. She had said that if we believed in Jesus Christ, Birju would get better in a minute. When she realized we were not going to convert, she took the hand lotion and talcum powder away.

Outside the church, I became giddy with relief. The wind was wet and cold. Walking across the parking lot, I laughed. "My God, I didn't know white people had such problems."

"Who are these people?" I said. "Who does things like that? Where are they from? Do they live in Edison? When they were talking, I kept thinking, *Why do you have problems? You're white. Even more terrible things should happen to you. You should suffer like Indians, like black people. That'll teach you.*" I said all this because I felt it. I also said it because I wanted my father to say he was nothing like the people in the meeting.

IN THE DAYS that followed, my father and I went to AA meetings every night. The meetings occurred in small rooms in churches and in big ones. Some took place in a very large, glass-walled party space that was next to a fire department. During the AA meeting, people drew curtains over these walls.

At first my father was regularly surrounded by men giving him their phone numbers. Some also gave him books and mimeographed sheets with lists of where the AA meetings took place. Surrounded by these people, I would feel scared, feel that we would have to say yes we wanted help, when in reality we wanted to be left alone.

I began to recognize some of the people from the meetings. Many of them appeared not just alcoholic but also crazy. There was a man who talked regularly about a religious radio station that he listened to. Another man, who carried a cane, would interrupt people as they spoke and offer his opinions. There was a very skinny woman who would say that she knew that the people in the meeting did not like her and then start crying.

Often as I sat in these meetings I was disgusted. Even the people who said sensible things, the men and women who shouted down the man who began passing out anti-abortion pamphlets, irritated me. They had created problems for themselves and their families with their drinking and now had to come up with such an elaborate solution that their families also had to be involved.

My FATHER, WHEN he got out of Bellevue, was nervous, timid. He would not look people in the eye.

In many ways, I don't think my mother and I realized how scared he was. A few weeks after he came home, he began telling people that we knew, people he saw on the train going to work, that he was an alcoholic, that he had been in a hospital because he couldn't stop drinking. Later, he told me and my mother that he did this because he hoped these people would somehow keep him from drinking.

My mother learned what my father was doing from her friend Mrs. Sethi. "Mr. Mishra must have been joking," Mrs. Sethi said apologetically. She was standing in the kitchen wearing jeans and a white shirt. "But you know, Shuba sister, what people are like. They gossip. They say bad things."

When I learned that my father had been telling people

about his drinking, I understood that he must have decided that how we were affected mattered less than whatever bene-fit he might gain. This filled me with shame.

The evening Mrs. Sethi visited us with the news, my mother shouted at my father in the kitchen. "You should have stayed in the hospital."

He stared at her without speaking, his eyes wet.

"People wouldn't spit on you if it weren't for me," she said.

A few days later, a financial planner visited. The man was somebody my father had told about being in Bellevue. Immediately this man had suggested that my father buy more insurance. "I couldn't say no," my father said to my mother.

"This is what happens. You showed him you were weak and so he thought, *Why not take advantage? He's an alcoholic. What somebody does to him doesn't matter.*"

The financial planner visited on a Sunday afternoon. He had floppy hair and wore a green suit that seemed large on him. My father brought him into Birju's room, where the nurse's aide was holding a bit of onion to Birju's nose as part of his sensory stimulation.

"If I drink and get into an accident, I need to protect him," my father said.

It sounded as if he was trying to win pity.

The financial planner had brought a large black binder with different booklets about insurance and investment funds. He spread these out for my father on the living room table. My mother, to express her suspicion and disgust, periodically came and stood in the doorway and stared disapprovingly.

As he talked, the financial planner kept touching my father's arm and knee. At the end of his visit, when he was about to leave, he said that the next step was for my father to give him power of attorney over his various accounts.

"No," my father said.

"Why not?" The man looked offended.

"Ji, I don't know you." The "ji" was a level of formality and politeness that showed how timid my father was at the time.

"What do you need to know? I can give you my phone number. I can give you my address. You're an alcoholic. You think you know more than me?"

WITHIN A FEW weeks of my father starting to tell people that he was an alcoholic, the news spread everywhere. One day at temple, Mr. Narayan came up to us and said to my mother, "Ji, you have to stop Mr. Mishra from saying these things. People get happy knowing that others are unfortunate."

First the doctors and engineers stopped visiting, then the middle-class people—the accountants and the shop owners. The last to stop were the people who lived in Hilltop Apartments, the ones who spoke neither Hindi nor English.

As the news spread and people stopped visiting, I began to feel shy around Birju. When I came into his room, I would

feel like we had failed him. I would remember how on my
first day at the nursing home I had sat by Birju and noticed
how quiet the home was compared to the hospital.

I KNEW THAT MINAKSHI would find out about my
father. I was scared of this. I had lied to her about him. I had
said that my father was cheerful, that he was a wall around
the family. He fought the insurance companies who didn't
want to pay. He managed the nurse's aides who were unre-
liable. I had said this because doing so made me look good.
Back then we Indian children, at least with each other, felt
that our value was to some extent based on our parents. If
our parents had gone to college, then we were a certain type
of child and were more valuable than someone whose parents
had not gone to college. It made sense, therefore, to praise our
parents. Also, we felt endangered by the world we lived in,
and so to speak ill of our protectors was to make the danger
more frightening.

Perhaps six weeks after my father began telling people on
the train that he was an alcoholic, the news finally reached
school. Minakshi came up to me at my locker. I was kneeling.
I looked up at her and my mouth went dry. I felt like I had
stolen from her. I was not from a good family but had convinced her I was, and she had come to my house and we had
lain in bed and she had let me rub against her.

I stood. Minakshi and I stared at each other.

"I don't like my father," she whispered.

Later that afternoon, as we stood among the trees and kissed, I was certain that there could be no better person than her.

Many of the boys at school disliked me. I was arrogant and annoying. I would boast about my grades while simultaneously whining about having to work. Vijay was very handsome. He was tall, which I envied, and he didn't have an accent. Vijay was smart and got good grades, but I was smarter and got better ones.

One morning, I was walking down a hallway and Vijay was walking toward me. He saw me and began to lurch from side to side. When he got to me, he reached out and dropped his hands on my shoulders. My heart jumped. Staring into my face, he slurred, "I am so drunk."

I pushed him away and, feeling blood pulsing behind my eyes, hurried off.

Vijay usually sat with the whites at lunch because he was on the cross-country team. Later that same day, he came to the Indian table at the cafeteria. He stood at one end, seven or eight chairs from me. He called out, "How is your dad? Is he feeling any better?"

I looked at my food. The table became silent.

"I hope he's feeling better."

Nobody spoke. After a moment, Vijay left. The table remained quiet. There was a minute or two of this silence and then when the boys and girls began talking again, they did not touch upon what had just occurred. I think this was because Vijay had embarrassed all of us. We were all a little shy about the lives we lived at home. At home we didn't eat the food that white kids ate. At home our mothers and some-times our fathers dressed in odd clothes. Our holidays were not the same as white people's. Our parents worshipped gods who rode on mice. To attack someone based on his or her family brought up so much of our own shame that we didn't have the heart to be mean.

Before we opened any of the letters, we prayed. My mother and I took whatever envelope had arrived that day and put it on the altar in my parents' room. The first response was from Brown University. The answer was no. We were kneeling before the altar. "It's OK," my mother said. She sighed and pushed herself off the floor. A part of me was ashamed to not have done something nice for my mother by getting into this famous university.

I stood. I also felt that I had been found out. I had the sense that Brown University knew all the wretched things about me, that I was not so smart, that in eighth grade, for a report on evolution, I had copied from an encyclopedia.

This and the other rejections came in March. I was now seventeen. We opened the envelopes when I got home from school. The air would be hard to breathe because my mother did her afternoon prayers around then and the incense smoke lingered.

Later, I learned that I was accepted into Princeton because

the short story I had submitted as part of my application was read by someone whose older brother had drowned.

My mother opened the letter. She tore off the side of the envelope and shook out the sheet of paper.

"Congratulations!" the acceptance began. I remembered kneeling at the temple in Queens and my mother opening the letter from the Bronx High School of Science.

"All your hard work has borne fruit," I blurted to my mother. "What you said you would do, you have done." I wanted no credit for what had occurred. To receive credit for getting into Princeton was to be responsible for having a life that would take me away from my family.

We went downstairs to tell Birju the news. My heart was racing. He was lying on his exercise bed. His stomach beneath his pajamas was swollen as if full of gas. The tube from his urinary catheter ran over his thigh to a bag that hung from the side of the bed. "We have fooled them," I said, taking hold of Birju's feet. "Brother mine, Mommy has done what she said she would. Get up, brother. How much longer can you keep lying here?"

THAT SPRING I was continuously aware that if the accident had not occurred, Birju would be graduating from college, that he would be applying to medical schools. The awareness was like a physical sensitivity, like when your back is hurting and you are careful all the time how you take a step.

Mrs. Sethi had been one of my mother's best friends. She had abandoned us. After my father's drinking became known, she had stopped talking to my mother, stopped visiting us or calling or returning my mother's phone calls. A part of me recognized that this made sense. Why spend time with strange, troubled, embarrassing people? Why seek problems? But the very fact that this made sense made my embarrassment worse.

Once I got into Princeton, people phoned and asked my mother to bring me to their homes. One of the ones who did this was Mrs. Sethi. She invited us to her house for dinner.

"Hello, sly one," she said, opening the door when we arrived. Because her husband was a dentist and they were prosperous, she could be a little more American than most people and she was wearing white pants and a blue silk blouse. I saw her and thought, *Now you're not ashamed to acknowledge us.*

Dinner was in a room that had an oval wooden table and cupboards with crockery along the walls. There was a chandelier above the table. My mother and I sat on one side of the table and Mr. and Mrs. Sethi on the other. Mr. Sethi was seated opposite my mother. He began the meal by saying, "Thank you for coming. We know it is difficult to leave Birju. We are flattered."

"If we wouldn't bother ourselves for you," my mother said, "who would we bother ourselves for?" My mother smiled broadly, angrily. She turned toward me. Her smile was fixed and was obviously false. "See what good manners Sethi uncle has, to thank someone for coming and eating at his house?"

There was a moment of silence.

Mrs. Sethi broke it by reaching to the center of the table where there were three steel pots. She lifted the lid off one and ladled chickpeas into a ceramic bowl. "Your mother said chickpeas are your favorite."

"Thank you," I murmured.

"See how good Sethi auntie is?" my mother said loudly and smiled her wide, angry, false smile.

Nobody spoke. We were all still for a moment and then slowly, arms and hands began reaching across the table. Bowls were filled, and a foil-wrapped stack of rotis was unpeeled, the bread passed around. We started eating. In the quiet, even the way my mother ate, tearing off pieces of roti and jabbing at the subji, seemed angry.

After several minutes, my mother turned to Mr. Sethi. She smiled and nodded as if agreeing with something he had just said, "Give him advice," she requested. "You know things about America that his father and I don't know."

Mr. Sethi looked embarrassed. He had a kind, meek face. "Ajay should keep doing what he's doing. He should help his parents and his brother."

"No. No. Give him guidance. Tell him what he needs to know if he is to get a good job." My mother leaned forward.

Mr. Sethi glanced at his wife as if asking what to do.

"Elder sister," Mrs. Sethi said, "We should turn to you

for guidance. You have raised a boy who has gotten into Princeton."

"What are you saying? We are lucky to be invited to a house like yours. After what Ajay's father did, I had no expectations." My mother's voice rose. Her anger was now in the open. We stopped eating.

"Sethiji, please give Ajay advice." My mother's voice was high and pathetic. "Please give him guidance."

Mr. Sethi glanced at me.

"Please," my mother said.

He nodded. "I didn't know this, Ajay, but in America the color of your belt is supposed to match the color of your shoes."

My mother leaned forward. "Tell him more," she said. "This is exactly the sort of thing he needs to know."

Mrs. Sethi said, "Shuba sister, all the important things you are already teaching him. These are the least important things."

My mother kept smiling and staring at Mr. Sethi. I felt bad for my mother.

"Learning to eat with a knife and fork is important," he said. "Before you get a job in America, before you get a good job, the person you will be working for often takes you to lunch or dinner, and then you need to know how to eat with a knife and fork."

"Wonderful. Wonderful," my mother said. "I would teach him such things, but I stay in the house all day."

"That's enough education for one night," Mrs. Sethi said.

My mother looked at her. "Please. The poor boy knows so little." She turned back to Mr. Sethi.

"Mrs. Mishra," Mrs. Sethi said, sounding irritated.

"I wish I could give him as good advice as your husband," my mother said, "but what can I do? My head is full of rubbish. I'm nobody."

"Why did you come if you wanted to fight?"

"How can you expect manners from me, Mrs. Sethi? My husband is a drunk."

Without finishing dinner, we left the house.

It was dark outside. A half moon that was a scrubbed white hung low over the rooftops. We stood for a minute in Mrs. Sethi's driveway. We had walked to the Sethis'. My mother opened her purse and took out a slender flashlight. She gave it to me. We started home. As we went down the sidewalk, my mother talked excitedly, angrily. "Even a cow has horns," she said.

Walking, I remembered that when we lived in India, the electricity would frequently go out at night, and my mother and I and Birju would be going someplace or coming back from someplace. My mother would then take a flashlight out of her purse and give it to Birju. Birju would walk ahead of us. He would guide us. He would wave the flashlight's beam over the ground. "Follow me," he would say.

Even when I left for college, shops had begun to open on the ground floors of the old houses that used to line Oak Tree Road where it enters Iselin. People ran businesses from their living rooms. The houses were pressed together and had narrow, fragile front porches that vibrated when you stepped onto them. The old white men and women who lived next door would pull aside their curtains to look at you when you arrived. Inside, there was usually a freezer that contained fish that someone had smuggled from Bengal. The shops carried packets of seeds for bitter gourd and the deep red carrots one finds in India and which are illegal to import. There would be old women in the back who didn't speak English and who prepared food for parties. Occasionally there was a child watching TV or doing homework.

In my first two years of college, some of the houses were gutted and made into ordinary stores. Others were torn down. I saw all this. I came home perhaps twice a month, bringing laundry and taking back food. I returned so often because my mother would phone crying. She would tell me that there had been no nurse's aides for seventy-two hours, that she was dizzy and vomiting from exhaustion. She would say, "Birju is bleeding out of his ass. Your father shouts at me when I say we should go to the hospital. He says that he won't put Birju on a respirator. I say, 'What does this have to do with a respirator?'"

My father continued not drinking. He was gloomier than ever, though. On weekends, he would shower and shave in the morning, put on fresh clothes, and then sit all day on the sofa in the living room, his arms crossed, his brow furrowed.

DIFFERENT PEOPLE IMMIGRATED now. Now one saw Indians working outdoors. There was a white-haired man who worked as a gas station attendant near my parents' house. Whenever I pulled in to his station and asked him how he was doing, he would start speaking quickly, eagerly about how much he hated America and every white person. I had the sense that if I told him that things were not so bad, he would hate me, too, and would think I only looked Indian but was as ignorant as a white.

These new immigrants were from chaotic backgrounds. I once saw two large, fat women punching each other in the mall.

The new immigrants went to temple, of course. They learned about us there and at the grocery stores. Some of them began to visit my mother. When I came home, women would bring their children to look at me. I would sit at the kitchen table doing homework. Their children would sit around me, looking shy.

My mother was happy to tell these women what to do. One woman's husband had a girlfriend. My mother wanted her to leave the man.

"Don't you think it makes her feel bad," my father said once, "when you tell her that if you were her, you'd pour gasoline over yourself and your children?"

PRINCETON IS FORTY-FIVE MINUTES from Edison. No matter how often I visited my parents, I felt that I was now in another country.

The Gothic buildings and the stone steps that were slick and beveled in the center from the generations walking on them made me feel that I was now a part of history. I had the feeling that if I was smart and behaved carefully, all good things would happen for me.

I had seven suitemates. Two were football players, one played ice hockey, and a fourth, golf. I tried fitting in. I bought Escher posters and one of Jimi Hendrix and put these on my walls.

I had been nervous about not doing well in college. During my first class, I looked at the notes the boy next to me was taking. His supply and demand curves seemed more neatly drawn than mine. Nearly everyone appeared to have gone to preparatory schools and already knew such odd things as the fact that there was no inflation during the Middle Ages. Very few, however, were willing to work the way I did.

When I would come out of Firestone Library at two in the morning, walk past the strange statues scattered around campus, and then sit at my desk in my room till the trees in the yard appeared out of the darkness, I felt that I was achieving something, that every hour I worked was generating almost physical value, as if I could touch the knowledge I was gaining through my work. One weekend, I came home to my parents and worked all Saturday night. In the morning, my mother saw me at my desk and brought me a glass of milk. Later, in Birju's room, she said to him, "Your brother can eat pain. He can sit all day at his desk and eat pain."

My first semester, I took a course on Shakespeare. Reading

When he shall die,
Take him and cut him out in little stars,
And he will make the face of heaven so fine
That all the world will be in love with night
And pay no worship to the garish sun,

I wished I loved Birju this way. Most of the course was devoted to strange, useless things, however—things like reading dreams that people of Shakespeare's time had written down in their diaries or letters. I majored in economics, focusing on econometrics.

MINAKSHI WAS IN college in Virginia. A phone call cost ten cents a minute if made after nine o'clock at night. To save money, we spoke every other day. On the days we didn't, I would call her room at nine and hang up after one ring. She would then do the same, and this was how we said we loved each other.

At the end of my freshman year, she told me that she had begun seeing another boy. I behaved the way people do in these cases. I would call her and cry and ask if she did the same things with the new boyfriend that she had with me. Sometimes at two or three in the morning, I would imagine she was with her boyfriend, and I would phone her to disturb their sleep.

Minakshi lives in Texas now. She is an accountant. This surprises me because you always expect people who matter a great deal to you to end up leading glamorous lives.

Near the end of my sophomore year, I began going out with a German girl. Back then, I automatically discounted anything a white person said. How could a white know what was true or real? I also felt jealous of white people. Diana sang in a chorus, and watching her sing made me angry. I would stand before her and sing in a mocking way. Diana started avoiding me after a few months. Finally she told me, "Stop

calling." I was so embarrassed by this that when she took a
semester off, I was relieved to not have her around campus.

AFTER I GRADUATED, I became an investment banker. I
had thought I was used to hard work. Now, I would leave the
office every morning when the coffee carts were being set up
on the sidewalk. I would return a few hours later during rush
hour. So little time would have passed since I left that when I
reentered the building, it would feel like the previous day was
continuing and, even though I had just showered and shaved,
I would have the strange feeling that I had put on new clothes
without having bathed.

In my first year as a vice president, I made seven hundred
thousand dollars. I found it very hard to spend money, however. One winter I needed to buy gloves, and because I didn't
want to pay what I thought was the premium that stores
charge for having to rent a building, I looked for somebody
selling gloves from a table on the sidewalk. I didn't see any
sidewalk vendors for several days, and so for those days I kept
my hands in my pockets.

Almost as soon as I started working, I began sending my
mother monthly checks. As I earned more, I sent her more.
My mother hoarded the money instead of spending it. "What
happens if you stop?" she said.

Periodically my parents came to see me in New York. I took them to places that I had started visiting, that I felt proud for visiting. Once, I took them to the Metropolitan Museum of Art. Most times, though, we went to fancy grocery stores. As we strolled through them, I remembered how when we first got to America, my mother used to take Birju and me through grocery stores, and we would stop to read the labels of the different types of canned food.

Birju had some white hair now. Often, after I had visited my parents and seen him, for days I would feel like I had been shouted at.

My mother started losing her hearing. She wanted to buy a hearing aid. "Why?" said my father. "If by mistake some good news does come for you, I'll write it down."

On my mother's sixtieth birthday, I gave her a check for a quarter of a million dollars. For a few days, she didn't cash it. She showed it to her friends. Then my parents began to have a nurse and a nurse's aide twenty-four hours a day. One afternoon when I came to their house, I found them sitting in lawn chairs in the backyard. I stood in the kitchen and watched them from a window.

For about seven years I didn't date in any sort of regular way. The stress of work was so enormous that I lost my temper easily. If I had dinner with a woman at a restaurant and she went to the bathroom, I became panicked. I felt that I had almost no time and the little I had was being wasted. Once, a woman took so long in the bathroom that I paid the bill and walked out. Another time, a woman I was at a movie with wouldn't leave when I didn't like the movie. I said, "I can't stay," and left.

I became sick with longing for women I barely knew. If a woman dressed well, I took this to signify that she could behave gracefully in every situation. I imagined not having much money and her still being kind.

Hema was a lawyer. I met her at a gathering of young Indian professionals. She was short and slightly stocky. She had wide hips, and she resembled one of those clay fertility goddesses one sees in museums. I had discovered that I liked what most women of my generation looked like, and whenever I saw her I became aroused.

I didn't know Hema well, but I took her to a resort in Mexico. On our first afternoon there, she went to the pool while I napped in our room. I came down around evening and went looking for her. The pool was enormous and softly blue. There was a white beach in the distance, and a red seaplane bobbing on the water. The pool area was noisy. People were talking, music was playing, and tables scraped against the cement patio as workers set up for dinner. It was the end of a beautiful day, warm and breezy.

I saw Hema and, standing by the side of the pool, waved to her. I was wearing shorts and a linen shirt. She kicked her way to me. She was wearing a blue swimsuit. I reached down and pulled her out of the water. She had a strong, solid body.

She leaned against me. "I'm tipsy," she slurred. Her pupils were dilated.

I walked her to a nearby table. She leaned heavily against me. "I got up too early this morning," she said.

Hema sat down on a wicker chair. She stretched her legs out and tilted her head back. She stared up at the darkening sky, her eyes wide and white. She looked beautiful. I began to get happy. I had a strange sense of everything being in its place. I turned away.

The last children were climbing out of the pool. People were laughing. In the distance a man and his family were walking off the beach. Dragonflies hung in the breeze. I felt sad, happy, content. The sun was setting. The wind was picking up. The fronds of the palm trees shivered in delight. I could feel the weight of Hema's body on the inside of my arm. I got happier and happier. In the distance was the beach and the breaking waves and the red seaplane bobbing in the water. The happiness was almost heavy.

That was when I knew I had a problem.

This book would not have been written without the help of numerous institutions and individuals.

The Mrs. Giles Whiting Foundation provided me with financial support when I was beginning to give up on the novel. The American Academy in Rome allowed me to stay in an apartment in their beautiful building when I was feeling especially wretched.

John Henderson, Ray Isle, and Nancy Packer read this manuscript numerous times. Bill Clegg was much more than an agent. Lorin Stein regularly suggested that I abandon this project and then, at the very end, helped drag the book over the finish line.

Most of all, I want to thank my editor Jill Bialosky and my publishing house W. W. Norton. When I handed it in, this book was nine years overdue. Each year, on the anniversary of the novel's due date, Jill would email me and invite me to lunch. I felt so ashamed for not having handed in the book that I would take weeks replying. Her patience and the patience of Norton make me feel that for years I have been in the company of extraordinarily kind people.